Boston Darkens

Boston Darkens

Michael Kravitz

Library of Congress Control Number: 2015918138
ISBN: Hardcover   978-1-5144-2252-6
                Softcover   978-1-5144-2251-9
                eBook   978-1-5144-2250-2

Print information available on the last page.

Rev. date: 11/05/2015

To order additional copies of this book, contact:
Xlibris
1-888-795-4274
www.Xlibris.com
Orders@Xlibris.com
717517

CONTENTS

IN LIFE WE all meet people who bring unnecessary drama. It's easy to complain and blame everything on others. Dealing with evil is not easy. It is to this end that I wish to dedicate this book to my brother, Barry. He recently lost his wife. They were both blessed with two sons. One son was born with multiple problems.

With so many problems, many parents would give up that child and make him a ward of the state. My brother's wife stayed home and spent day and night caring for her son. She herself developed many medical problems. With trust in God and herself, she cared for her ill son. Her son lived many years past what the doctors gave her. He finally succumbed in his twenties. My brother's wife passed away spring of 2015.

Soon after the funeral, I informed my brother that I was writing this novel. My brother's will to go on has inspired me to finish my novel. He read each section and edited several grammatical errors. His wife was a writer, and she helped too. Through this novel I am reaching out to all for humanity and hope.

CHAPTER 1

Introduction

YOUNG PEOPLE ARE sitting in a sidewalk café in Israel, enjoying stimulating conversation. In a split second, a bomb blast destroys their lives. A train ride in Spain carries people to work and tourists to their next sight. A bomb goes off, and the train derails. In Nigeria, a young Christian family has to battle poverty and government corruption. They send their little girl to an all-girls school. There she can receive a good education and learn about morality and showing kindness to all things. The next day the parents are horrified that hundreds, including their own child, are taken in the name of religion. In Kenya, one of the Swahili sister countries, terrorists invade a defenseless mall. The Christian shoppers are separated. They are then executed one by one.

Even despots like Putin, Kaddafi, and Mubarak understood the horrible persecutions. In their own strong ways, they protected many minority religions. Our mainstream news never seems to report the whole truth.

Somehow Americans seemed oblivious to these events. TV, sports, and the hustle of everyday life seemed to say, "Not over here." See no evil, hear no evil, then I guess there is no evil. In the last several years, there have been multiple attacks. Most so far have to do with our military. They fight our wars so that we can be free. When they return stateside, they are not armed. They are easy targets for those schooled in hatred. The Internet and preaching in certain religious venues has stroked the flames of hatred.

In an open society as ours, there are multitudes of soft targets. Our water, transportation, shopping, and any gatherings of people are soft targets. Yet to me the most devastating form of destruction is an EMP nuke. A rogue missile from a terrorist group could set it off high above us.

The economic and human destruction would be a game changer. For several billion dollars, we can protect our grid.

We've known about EMPs (electromagnetic pulses), also described as transient electromagnetic disturbances, for decades. When a changing electromagnetic field crosses a wire, an electric current is generated in the wire. It is the basic phenomena used in electric generators. Some nuclear bombs are designed to produce a series of gigantic electromagnetic spikes or pulses. When they cross the wires on any unshielded electric device, the generated electric spikes fry the devices sensitive internal circuitry.

Because so many countries have the ability to detonate nuclear devices, the dangers of EMPs are real, and these can destroy parts or even all of our power grid. Many scientist and politicians have warned congress. Rep. Trent Franks, a Republican from Arizona, has stated the possibility of destruction to computers, water, and electronic devices.

There has been a rise in terrorism both from abroad and at home. Many Americans and people all over the world sense the tension. We have witnessed a number of attacks in the United States, Europe, Russia, and the Middle East.

Fiction writers have concentrated on the drama surrounding the possibilities of various attacks. Not all but most take you to a remote area. Here is where we find the survivalist struggle against all odds to continue on. I have elected to be more pragmatic, zooming down on one certain family in the outskirts of Boston. New York, Boston, and the Pentagon among others have seen their share of tragedy. The FBI, CIA, and many local authorities are working tirelessly to prevent as many attacks as possible.

Ben Randal and his wife, Alice, have been blessed with the American dream. They have two children, Jessica and Randy. Both Ben and Alice have good jobs, and they raised their children in a traditional American Christian home. They are from Nebraska, and they found the culture and customs of the East Coast a little challenging. Their faith, character, and resolve are put to an extreme test.

I chose to be pragmatic in the way I have portrayed politicians, foes, and allies. Both the good and evil of people come out when they are under threat. There is also the problem of anonymous mob behavior of fearful, ill-informed crowds of people who live in any large city like Boston or New York.

With a little dry humor and some heart-stopping tension, I have waded into the drama of a post-EMP attack. It is the story of Ben

Randal, his family, his neighbors, and some quirky friends coming together with some old-fashioned values and hope as they struggled to survive.

I have attempted to keep you, my reader, entertained. I hope you enjoy reading this story as much as I have enjoyed writing it.

CHAPTER 2

Tribal Water

MY SON, RANDY, handed me a crowbar and a three-foot hose. I was a little worn down mentally, and so I responded with a disconnected, "Huh?"

"Earth to Dad. You'll be needing it on the trip."

"Um, thanks, son. Guess I got lost looking at your car."

There was film on the windows and dirt on the floors of his 1956 Buick. It was unlike Randy to let his vintage car be anything but pristine. He was fully employed as a grease monkey about twelve miles from home. Randy had chosen a different road from the rest of the family. I had tried to instill in him the importance of reading and going on to college; however, being a good student came too easily for him. He found no passion in it. Vintage cars, on the other hand, stirred him. Those did provide passion in his life. I mused on, *Ever since Randy was a little boy—*

"Dad!"

"Sure, son. I was just inspecting your car. Have to make sure that it is all set for the trip. You know, your sister, Jessica, and her friend Vivian are going to join me, and they aren't mechanics."

"Sure, Dad."

I grew up in the Midwestern part of the country, rural Nebraska to be more precise. Attitudes were different there. One learned to be independent in order to survive. Calling a repairman for service was unheard of, even if one could find one within three hours of where we lived. You learned to work hard, fix things yourself, and make your own decisions.

Mostly I made good ones. Back then drugs weren't the problem that they are today. Booze was a bit difficult to come by but not impossible for an inventive young fella. I made a decision early on—based on some personal experience, I must admit—that the hangover thing was no fun at all. Occasional social drinking was okay. I just didn't like genuflecting to that damn porcelain god.

Out in Nebraska, football and wrestling were the real gods. I tried football, but at six feet and 170 pounds, I wasn't going to bowl anyone over. It would have taken a superhuman effort to become really good on the football field or the wrestling mat. I just wasn't that interested. So I turned to my natural inclination to understanding how things worked. I focused on biology and math at school, and I went on to college and even grad school.

Then I worked for a biotech company. Even though the work was intense, I was fairly good at it. To get an emotional release, I returned to old, comfortable habits like fixing my appliances or working on my Honda Accord. My attitude must have been more relaxed at these times because Randy often joined in to help me. Guess the apple didn't fall far from the tree.

I started the Buick up. "Be careful," Alice said to Jessica.

"Mom, I'm with Dad and Vivian. I'm fine." Seating in the back was tight. We had thirty empty water bottles. We tied them in tens. I kept my .22 rifle and few boxes of ammo near me. It had been seven days since the EMP nuke had gone off.

The old car sounded great. They didn't have all those computerized ignition systems. They weren't as sensitive to the effects of an EMP blast. Still, the old mechanical thermostat wasn't working right, and so we wore warm clothes. April is a mixed-up month weather-wise in the Boston area.

After he left the house, we started down the road. Fortunately we were in a rural area, and we only needed to dodge a few stranded cars. "That's Fred's dad's car," Vivian said softly, trying to hide her presence. Jessica quietly sat next to her, twirling her own hair. I guessed that at seventeen, they were both in the midst of some stage of insecurity.

"Look, girls, there's no electricity, and we are not on a social mission. So speak up. This whole situation is new to me too." I was never too good at understanding the whys of teenage girls. Jessica was always insecure and nervous around boys. Vivian was an African-American teenager, sensitive and easy to be with. Their conversations often seemed consumed with talk about their futures and, of course, boys.

Around the next bend was Route 95, which headed toward Providence. "Yikes!" exclaimed Vivian. "Look at all those cars."

"God," I muttered. "Now I have to go over the curb and onto the grass."

"Watch the car," Jessica said. "Randy will go ape shit if we damage it."

"Please, Jessica, stop. We're off to Connecticut."

"Why so far away, Dad?"

"There will be fewer people who know about the spring water outlet there," I said firmly. "Look, girls, both Mom and I have been listening to the survival radio. Your grandpa had a lot of interesting stuff."

Jessica now had a stern look. "You mean that right-wing kook."

"He had his ways," I said justly.

"Yeah, right," Jessica said distinctly. "He was always listening to those talk shows on the radio and shouting."

"Jessica, he's gone, all right? We have his radio, survival kit, MREs, a .22 rifle, a first-aid kit, and a lot more."

"Sorry, Dad. You're right." Jessica had never warmed up to Grandpa, but she did have a soft spot for Grandma, who was now in a Boston hospital.

We were within ten miles of Providence, Rhode Island. Abandoned cars were everywhere. A few people were trying to push them to the side. Route 95 was also littered with clothes, grocery bags, and a few corpses of those who didn't make it. Vivian was sniffling. "Those poor people. Why can't the authorities help?"

"Police cars and ambulances also stopped," I said with some compassion. "They use whatever they've got that still works—horses, bicycles, and a few vintage cars. That's all."

We hit a patch were we were driving in the breakdown lane. We were passing hundreds of cars, many with broken windows. It was obvious many looters were looking for anything they could get. The three of us looked on with astonishment. The whole scene looked like it had been lifted out of some video game for teenage boys.

"Christ!" I said loudly. "I'll bet my new Honda Accord has broken windows. It died on the Mass Pike. Damn, just three miles from the company parking lot and forty-five more payments. Well, Vivian, you think the postman will be delivering a late payment notice?"

"Yeah, Dad, and they'll bring their vintage tow truck," Jessica said jokingly. Vivian smiled and stopped fiddling with her hair. The tension had lifted for a moment. But the happy mood did not last long. As we approached Providence, we heard a loud roaring noise overhead. "What was that?" shouted Jessica. We were all frightened. I pulled over and got out of the car. The girls couldn't stop shaking.

"What's going on?" Jessica said, even louder.

"Quiet!" I insisted. The two jets had turned, and now they were coming back over Route 95. "Russian Migs." *But why?* I wondered. "Looks like they flew over toward Boston and back to the Atlantic Ocean. Has to be a reconnaissance flight." They did not return.

As we drove farther, a couple on bicycles stopped. I rolled down the window.

A young man commented, "That was scary. We are trying to get some news, but there is very little coming out. It seems that beyond the Plains states, they were not affected."

"Isn't that ironic?" I muttered.

"What do you mean?" the puzzled bicyclist asked.

"My wife and I settled for the Boston area instead of California. The idea of wildfires, mudslides, earthquakes, and water shortages didn't appeal to us."

When we said good-bye to our new friends, I saw a twinkle in Jessica's eye. *They're a little too old and refined for her,* I thought. Cars were now really presenting a cluster problem. I drove mostly in the breakdown lane, where there were only a few cars that had been pushed to the side. It was sad to see the vandalism. *Punks. They never get it.*

We approached the split between 95 and 195. One headed to Cape Cod, and the other went to Connecticut. "Damn, Dad, you always got your spring water at Cape Cod," Jessica quipped.

"Yes, but there are hundreds of people from Wareham, Hyannis, and Falmouth going there. On the survival radio, your mom heard there are riots and even a few shootings."

The corridor between New York City and Boston is heavily traveled. It seemed 95 was always under construction. At Providence, the 95 and 195 interchange had been completely revamped. As it sat next to the Atlantic Ocean, there were a limited number of roads leading to Providence. Traffic during rush hour was heavy. The landscape was littered with cars, trucks, motorcycles, and debris. Parking lots were generally clean, but this looked like a *Mad Max* wasteland.

As I weaved on, I saw a wrinkled face on Vivian. I knew she felt stressed. As we passed I- 195, I had to ease her anxiety. "Look, Vivian."

"What, Mr. Randal?" Vivian struggled to say. She was hiding thoughts of better times.

"You remember the movie *Dumb and Dumber*?"

"Yes, Mr. Randal," she said with more authority and curiosity.

I continued, "That is where the big blue bug was advertising a pesticide company. It was an easily recognized landmark. Travelers always remembered when they were passing it."

Jessica half-smiled. "That dead parrot scene in *Dumb and Dumber* was funny."

"I do not like to see any innocent animal die," Vivian proclaimed with sadness.

Providence Bay seemed like driving the New Jersey Turnpike. There was a cluster of large gas tanks and tall piles of coal and treated sand. (During the winter they would use it on icy roads.)

In the middle of this commerce area was a gentleman's club. Here the working man or junior executive could waste his hard-earned money on expensive drinks while scantily clad women pressured them to buy even more. I guess they put the club there because of zoning.

When I looked in the rearview mirror, I could see that Jessica and Vivian seemed a little less tense. After another ten minutes down 95, I saw signs for T. F. Green Airport. You buy a plane ticket to Providence, but the airport is really in Warwick, Rhode Island. I guess saying Providence sounds richer than saying Warwick. Warwick is like Salem, your quaint New England town. It conjures up images of white Puritans, red Indians, and witches—the images that the vendors use for Halloween costumes.

As we were going under the overpass near Exit 14, Jessica shouted, "Oh, my God." I slowed down. It is hard to dodge stalled vehicles and look. On the left, there was an elderly man and a woman who were being hassled by ten to twelve young punks. Now at a dead stop, I put my hand on my .22 rifle.

The leader seemed to be this skinny, tall kid. He had a Mohawk haircut. He was unshaven, and he was clothed in dirty blue jeans, work boots, a flannel shirt. I saw that he had a 9mm gun. Two others also had guns. One was a short man. He seemed meek in nature, and he stood about five-foot-six.

The other gave off vibes like an angry bitch, consumed by some injustice forced upon her person. She was almost as tall as the skinny man but a lot heavier. Easily weighing 190 pounds, she had a short haircut, and wore no makeup. Her outfit was made up of a black leather jacket with silver buttons, loose dungarees, sneakers, and a condescending attitude.

The elderly couple drove up in a yellow Mustang. The old lady showed no fear. She was scolding the leader. *Decision time*, I thought. I had a responsibility to my daughter and Vivian. I also had to come back alive to sustain my son and wife. Two neighbors were also counting on me. What a quandary. I needed to show my daughter and Vivian that I was in charge. I needed to show confidence, but the moment was filled with fear and indecision.

We were on the other side of the highway. The old lady and the leader were in a heated exchange. At the next moment a chill ran down my spine. The angry lady in black leather slowly turned her head and looked at our car. I held my .22 a little tighter. My adrenalin started to run.

God sure worked in mysterious ways. At that tense moment, Jessica called out and tugged at my coat. "Dad. Hey, Dad."

"What Jessica?" I never let my eyes off the angry bitch.

"Dad, let's keep going."

"We are on the wrong side of the road. We're on a mission, remember?"

"You're right."

I started to go slowly forward, the whole time keeping an eye on the angry bitch.

The traffic was jammed, and for the sake of mental survival, my thoughts drifted toward my son's Buick. It was a 1956 Buick Riviera splashed all over with a bright red color. He came across this classic in Nebraska when we lived in a rural farming town. We were friends with the Hestons. They were simple folks living on social security, and they also earned a few dollars with a small crop of potatoes. They drove an old 1963 Chevy pickup truck. Mr. Heaton also had a 1956 Buick just sitting in the backyard. Three tires were flat, and it seemed to have a lot of rust. When Mr. Heaton passed on, Mrs. Heaton offered the car to Randy for a low price. He jumped on the offer. She needed the funds for Mr. Heaton's funeral. When we relocated to Massachusetts, Randy had his car shipped there.

To me, it was a money pit. To Randy, it was a piece of priceless artwork. He could have been a lawyer, an accountant, or an engineer, but he elected to be an auto mechanic. I'm glad because now the Buick was our lifeline.

My mind woke up from its peaceful thoughts of the bright red Buick and old Chevy pickup trucks. We were already at Exit 13 on Route 95. Usually it took less than forty minutes to the Connecticut border. Though he had to dodge stalled cars, I had hoped it would take just an hour. There were fewer cars that littered the road. The farther from Providence, the less cars we encountered. Most of the time driving in the breakdown lane was smooth. After a few minutes, we came to Route 295. It is the outer beltway around Providence. During rush-hour traffic or major traffic jams, 295 is an alternate way to bypass Providence. Soon I saw Route 4 on the left. It is the split that goes to the beaches and Route 1. To me, it was a sigh of relief. We were getting close to the Connecticut border.

We passed by an abandoned eighteen-wheeler that was almost brand new. *Lord*, I thought, *that is a big truck.* The value of the truck and its contents must be worth hundreds of thousands. *Money*, I thought. *What value does that have now?* Food, water, and medical supplies are all that had any meaning now. Survival was all that mattered for my family. Then my train of thought was interrupted.

"Dad," Jessica spurted out. "Dad," she said in a louder voice.

"What, honey?" I looked in the rearview mirror.

"I have to tinkle. The water we have been drinking doesn't agree with me."

"All right, honey. Hold on." I pulled up next to a 2012 Chevy Blazer. When I looked at the gas gauge, it was down to a quarter of a tank. I stopped the Buick.

Vivian replied softly. "Yes" if she wanted to go with Jessica.

I always thought it was odd that women went to the bathroom together. God, if I said that to a friend, it would be "whoa get away from this dude."

"I need a little water for my hands," Jessica said with authority."

"Be careful with how much you use."

"Yes, Dad," Jessica said sweetly.

"You too, Vivian."

"Yes, Mr. Randal," Vivian said with respect. The girls went off to the side of the road just beyond my sight.

Now the fun starts, I thought. I went into the trunk, and then I got the crowbar and the hose. With some of the newer cars, you needed to open the gas cap from the inside. I still had the Midwest upbringing in me. My dad always said, "The good Lord watches your every movement." I needed the gas, but I did not want to damage the car. I got the gas cap opened, and then I sucked on the hose. "Yuck," I said. Nothing was worse than the taste of gas. I got the air out of the hose.

Gas was flowing down. "Crap," I said. "Now what do I do?" I couldn't put it directly in my tank—I would lose the siphon connection. So I capped my end with a piece of plastic and a screwdriver. Now it was airtight.

At this point I collected myself. I had a funnel, but I needed a container. I would hate to use one of the empty water bottles. Water bottles were precious. The girls came back and saw me in my bewildered state.

"What's up, Mr. Randal?" Vivian asked with a little stress in her voice.

After several minutes we heard a small engine. It was a man on an old Harley motorcycle. He looked to be in his forties. He was somewhat tall, and he weighed a good two hundred pounds. Even his helmet and clothes seem to come from a far-off vintage year. As he approached closer, the girls and I became apprehensive. I felt a little unsure how to handle this. My mind was racing. I had to quickly determine if he was a threat to us. I knew the girls would not do well without me. I was sure my wife and son also depended on our mission.

I took my rifle out of the car. Instead of holding it in my hands, I just put the butt end of the rifle on the pavement. To me, this was a "trust but verify" gesture. As long as he didn't go for his rifle, neither would I. We were all a little anxious. As he got closer he slowed down and stopped about twenty feet from us. The kickstand came out. He kept a close eye on my rifle. "How are we doing?" he asked.

"We are doing just fine," I said confidently.

"My name is Vincent," the motorcyclist said with a friendly voice, slowly gazing at the two girls. He bowed his head and then proceeded to take his rifle out with his left hand. He laid the rifle down and slowly walked a good ten feet away. Then he said, "Look, man, I have my own mode of transportation, and you have yours. I also need gas. I'm below a quarter of a tank. Your hose is not going to work without a container."

"Jessica," I said.

"Yes, Dad," she said with compliance.

"Please hold my rifle."

"Yes, Dad."

I took the crowbar and nodded to Vincent. "Okay, Vince. Is it all right to call you Vince?"

"Sure," the motorcyclist replied.

"Great. You can call me Ben. It is short for Benjamin. Benjamin Randal."

"Got it," said the motorcyclist. "I will take these three cars, and you can take those two." Vincent went to his Harley and grabbed a flat-head screwdriver.

Several minutes later Vince yelled, "I think we got one." At this point I started to walk over to Vince. I turned slowly toward Jessica and gave a small nod. Jessica grabbed the rifle and put her finger on the trigger. The rifle was on her lap and out of sight.

As I got closer, Vince said, "Look in the backseat. Two gallons of fruit juice, baby wipes, and a three roll of paper towels."

"Okay, Vince. Let's open this car with minimal damage," I said with authority. Vince pried the window with the screwdriver. I took the crowbar and tried to lift the latch, but after a few minutes, I wanted to break the window.

"Yo, man, be cool. We got this." Vince went back to his cycle and unwrapped the wire that held his bed pack. Without hesitation, he made a loop at the end of the wire. He again pried the window. "Hand me your crowbar, Ben," he said with a little impatience. He took the crowbar and bent the window more. "Ben, just hold the crowbar like this." I guess there was a new sheriff. As I held the crowbar, Vince opened the latch on the first try.

As he gazed at the two girls, Vince commented. "Heh, man, we make a good team." I half-smiled. I knew he did not want to humiliate me in front of the girls. "Look, man, we got to rinse these bottles out with a little of your water."

"Okay," I replied. We were close to our water outlet. Vince and I filled the bottles and then shared the spoils. He filled his before I filled mine.

Vince then said, "Look, man, let's get you up and running."

I felt less intimidated. "Where you headed, Vince?"

"Lyme, Connecticut. I came from Salem. My Dad passed away two and a half years ago. I am nervous. There is no way my mom can survive."

At this point I told Vince about our watering hole. "Thanks, man, but I need to move on," he said politely. "God has plans for all of us. I just hope he spares my mom. She is all I have." He put his hand over his face to mask his tears. After he put his kickstand up, he ended with the words, "God be with you." He started his cycle and drove off without looking back.

"That's a man on a mission," I said to Jessica and Vivian. *Sure could use a few friends like that*, I thought. "Okay, girls, let's blow this pop stand."

"How much farther, Dad?" Jessica said with impatience.

"We are within twenty minutes form the Connecticut border. From there it is maybe another ten minutes." The cars were fewer in numbers. We reached Exit 1. It was the last exit in Rhode Island. We descended downward, and now we could see the state border. Most of the visitors to Casino Woods followed the little signs. They pointed to another exit that led away from our watering hole. As we got off 95, we came to a stop sign.

"Look, Jessica. This is where I use to buy fireworks." There were several places to buy them within a quarter of a mile

"Why are they closed, Dad?" Jessica ask.

"I am not totally sure, but they are illegal in Rhode Island and Massachusetts."

The Rhode Island State Troopers would normally see the cars coming on 95. The exit was within eyesight of their perch. For five to six weeks before the Fourth of July, they stopped cars. If they caught you, you would lose your purchase and incur a fine. Most customers from Massachusetts went to New Hampshire. There were multiple back roads. The survival rate was better up there.

Now we were very close. "Dad, why did you come all this way?"

"What are you getting at, Jessica?"

"We have some small casinos in Massachusetts."

"That's true, Jessica, but they are fairly new and small. The politicians have their hand in everyone's pocket. Massachusetts is a one-party state. The joke is you can fit all the Republicans in a clown car. In last few elections, there was a little increase in the affluent areas. There are always objections from the churches and progressive activists. Besides, Jessica, Foxwoods is larger. The alcoholic drinks are free. The waitresses are nicer."

"You mean they are pretty."

"I didn't say that, Jessica."

"Men, they are so shallow" Jessica retorted with a little sarcasm.

"Uh-huh, you got that right, girl" Vivian said in agreement. There was no use fighting it. I just kept quiet. There was activity around the bend. There were several vintage vehicles, bicycles, wheelbarrows, carts, and even a horse.

"Are we there, Dad?" Jessica asked excitedly.

"Yes, we are, Jessica." There was a line of about twenty people. It was mixture of locals and Pequot Indians. A water pipe that came out of the hillside had a sign from the Board of Health that said "This water is not authorized or tested by the Board of Health!"

During the past ten to fifteen years, I often saw the locals and the Pequot's fill their plastic containers here. It was ironic. When I noticed the old vintage cars and trucks, I used to feel sad for them. Now without modern EMP sensitive electronics, they are the ones remaining on the roads.

When one traveled down this country road, the economic struggle was apparent. The houses needed repair. The barns, trucks, and tractors were vintage. It really reminded me of old Nebraska. Even though the economic struggle was real, the people were of solid character.

As the casino opened, the money ventures swooped in, attempting to buy as much as they could. Slowly hotels, gas stations, and coffee shops sprang up. Town fathers kept the zoning tight. "This is not Las Vegas. This is the land of the Pequot and Puritans." Their buildings fit the integrity of the landscape. I always felt good that many of them did not sell out. The license to build the casino did go to the tribe. Many became rich, which was good for them. In the beginning many of the dealers and pit bosses were Pequot. As Foxwoods grew, the percentages changed.

I pulled the Buick off to the side of the road and asked the girls, "Do you want to fill the bottles or guard the Buick?" Jessica felt squeamish about using the rifle to stand guard. "Vivian and I will do the filling."

I noticed a poster with the number six written on it. It stood more than two feet tall and two feet wide. The girls took four bottles each and stood in line behind a Pequot Indian father and son. The son was in front. His pants were blue jeans, and his shirt was tribal. In his belt Jessica saw a long hunting knife. The father was five-foot-ten and maybe 190 pounds. His attire was tribal with a loose-fitting shirt over his pants.

As the girls settled in, the father turned his head slowly to the left. He made a slight glance toward Jessica and muttered in a low, masculine voice. "Hmm, white man took our land. White man brings us his diseases. Now white man brings his war machine." Both Jessica and Vivian bowed their head in fear. Once more he looked back and noticed Vivian. "Hmm," he said with a slight smile. He probably misjudged Jessica. Her good friend was African American. Maybe this met with his approval.

The water pipe looked like it was jerry-rigged. There was no concrete basin or any elaborate fittings. It was a simple pipe that had been driven into the hillside. One simply put out a water container to collect spring water.

April often produced afternoons as cloudy and cool as this one. It had been a harsh and snowy winter. The last two to three years the winters seemed to get worse. Cape Cod had always been known for winter golf, but the new weather patterns changed that. Jessica and

Vivian were mostly quiet. The mood was resolute and somber. No one seemed to smile or talk.

The only two who seemed different were two young New Yorkers who arrived in a spiffy Edsel. *I bet that the storage fee for that beauty is hefty*, I thought. Its backseat and trunk were filled with empty water bottles. New York City from this point was a good three-and-a-half-hour drive. They looked like people who made six-figure salaries. My guess was that they were either lawyers or marketing execs. One wore black pants with white stripes, and the other wore light tan khaki pants. *God, don't they ever give up*, I thought. I knew New Yorkers often made fashion statements, but at this point, who cared?

An older couple with six containers just finished. The New Yorkers had been impatiently waiting their turn, making remarks about how they had traveled the farthest and deserved to fill up all they wanted. They seemed insensitive to the others around them when their turn started. The one is khaki pants filled four bottles, brought them to the Edsel, and then returned with eight more empties while the one in black pants filled up two more.

The young Indian son spoke up. "Sign says six. You fill up to six and go back of the line."

Black Pants looked at him, brushed back his coat, and responded, "Yeah, right." He then returned to filling up his water bottles. You could cut the tension in the air with a knife. The father put his hand on his son's back. He stepped to the side and spoke with his deep voice.

"Sign says six. This territory is ours. These are our ways. If you don't like them, leave." He brushed his tribal shirt to the side, showing a much larger gun than the New Yorkers carried. At this point everyone was getting nervous.

Although I was a good hundred feet away, I had to act to prevent any unnecessary violence. I grabbed my rifle and ran for the first fifty feet with the barrel pointed down. Now I walked at a fast clip and yelled out, "Do we have a problem here?" The two New Yorkers looked at me to size up the situation.

"No, there is no problem." They put aside all but the original plastic containers. Still pointing my barrel, I gazed at the father. He looked back at me. We did not utter any words. He simply let his tribal shirt cover his gun. I walked slowly back to the Buick. Every few feet I glanced at the two New Yorkers but not at the father. I decided to sit on the hood of the Buick and keep the rifle on my lap. It was now the father and son's turn. They walked back with their full quota. Jessica and Vivian began to fill their quota.

The two New Yorkers were back in line with more empties. They did not stare at either the Pequot Indians or me. Instead they kept quiet this time. The father looked at the Edsel. He noticed that the two New Yorkers were only halfway done. His son finished putting the water bottles in the bed of the old Chevy. The son yelled out," All set, Pop. Time to go."

The father said. "You can go. I think I will stay for a while." The son slowly glanced over at the line and the two New Yorkers.

"Well, Pop. Nothing good on TV. I think I will stay here with you." It took close to an hour and a half before the New Yorkers filled all their bottles. Jessica and Vivian were now finished with ours. We were about to leave when the father came to me with corn. As he handed me some, he politely said, "For a white man, you're not bad."

"We have plenty of corn." I thanked him.

Jessica piped up, "Didn't the Pilgrims encounter the same? In their first winter, they lost half of their population. It was the Indians who gave them food and saved their lives. But afterward they were not treated the same way."

Vivian now joined in, "Hey, Jessica, do you remember that statement we heard in history class, the one about the *natural way*? You know, the one from Luther Standing Bear, a chief of the Lakota peoples? I always liked it. He said, 'Conversation was never begun at once, or in a hurried manner. No one was quick with a question, no matter how important, and no one was pressed for an answer. A pause giving time for thought was the truly courteous way of beginning and conducting a conversation.'"

The Pequot Indian father turned and looked at Vivian, waiting until he caught her attention. He smiled at her and then looked over toward the New Yorkers and said, "They not know Luther Standing Bear." Before he turned to walk away, he leaned in, faced Vivian, and whispered, "Way to go, girl. Hmm." Then he flashed her a quick thumbs-up and walked away.

The moment was too good, but I was still fighting the urge to laugh out loud. If I did, however, I reasoned that old Luther's speech would rat me out too.

Jessica, Vivian, and I got in the old Buick. We were glad to be on the way home. Jessica soon said, "Dad, is there any way we can cook some of this corn?"

Normally I would just ignore the comment or say, "Not now, Jessica." But I felt hungry too, so I replied, "We'll see, Jessica."

With the spoils in the car, we drove back toward Rhode Island. As we approached the intersection, I saw a concrete slab again. It had once been a fast-food chain that had closed. People had torn down the building and left the slab there. I instinctively turned the Buick. We drove up the hill seventy-five feet and stopped the Buick next to the slab. I said to the girls, "Let's look for paper and twigs to build a fire." After a few minutes, we had enough material to build a fire.

Like a good Boy Scout member, I soon had the fire blazing. We found some longer twigs. Instead of marshmallows, we roasted corn. We took out one bottle of fresh springwater and enjoyed the feast. "Burnt corn. It really tastes good," I stated to Jessica. "Well, we went on our camping trip."

"Yeah, Dad, we surely did."

"Vivian, are you all right?" I asked. She, too, enjoyed the corn.

"Yes, Mr. Randal," she said softly. "I miss my mom. I have three sisters, Mr. Randal. My mom raised all of us by herself." At this point I did not know what to say. I kept quiet. Vivian's mom didn't get any help from their fathers. "My mom wears a big cross on her neck. Every night she prays to Jesus. She never did drugs or stole. She wants me to break the chain." At this point I was curious.

"You have a nice family, Mr. Randal. All of you help each other and work. My mom wants me to get out of the ghetto life. She wants me to study hard and be like your family."

"What do you want to do, Vivian?" I asked politely.

"I want to be a lawyer. I am on the honor role. Now I don't know if we will even survive. There are so many hardships. I really wish I could call her. Less than a year, and then this happens. I studied so hard. I really want to make my mom proud. My dad was never there for me. Two years ago he contacted me and informed me he had terminal cancer. I felt bad, but I didn't really know him. In his last year, he got me a cell phone. He had very little money. He wanted to make peace. I wish I knew him better. My mom always says I need to let it go. It just can't end like this. It can't."

MICHAEL KRAVITZ

Vivian started to cry. Jessica hugged her. "We love you, Vivian. We're here for you."

At this moment I realized that I was really bonding with my daughter. I did not want the moment to end. Jessica then said to Vivian. "Let's tinkle before starting back."

What a mood breaker, I thought.

As the girls went behind the bushes, I put out the fire and gazed down at the road. There was unusual traffic. People were carrying their empty water bottles. They used wheelbarrows, carts, bicycles, and even a horse. The horse had the bottles strapped to both of its sides. I wish I had a camera. This is like an American version of the Ho Chi Minh Trail.

As we started off in the Buick, we noticed a Dunkin' Donuts shop. Jessica said, "Can we get a Coolatta?"

"Sure, honey." It was weird. There were six cars there but no people. The door looked opened. We just kept going. People had ransacked most stores and markets. At least the ones that were within walking distance.

At the intersection we took a right and quick left. There were only a few cars and one motorcycle in the way. We were now heading north on Route 95 heading north. Rhode Island was within sight. It was early afternoon, and it had already been a long and trying day for all of us. I kept thinking of the sitcom *Gilligan's Island.* They were only going on a three-hour cruise when disaster struck.

Our day was not over. We were in uncharted times. Old habits were hard to break. I kept thinking that I needed to call my wife and let her know everything was all right. I feel very insecure without my phone. My mom would always say, "When you leave, make sure your wallet has money and a AAA card in it, and be sure you have a cell phone." Now all I could do is send up smoke signals. But who would see them?

We were now in Rhode Island, heading north on 95. The girls and I were getting anxious. It was already midafternoon. Normally at this point we would be home in less than hour. But these are not normal times, and every stalled vehicle had its own story. Stoically we pushed on. We saw stalled vehicles and also motorcycles that had met their demise with tragedy. It was a battle zone where unleashed dogs and other animals searched for food.

I looked in the rearview mirror and tried to put the watering hole behind me as a distant memory. After a good twenty-minute drive, we came upon an unusual sight—a bread truck and a young man with a screwdriver. *My God*, I thought. *What is he going to accomplish with that?* He was slight in physique, and I assumed he had arrived by the bicycle next to him.

Sitting on the grass nearby was a young woman who acted the part of his significant other. She looked like a duck out of water. She was wearing fine blue jeans, a button-down blouse, and fancy sneakers. The bicycle was a woman's bike with wide tires and a basket attached to the front. It was obviously meant for short distance jaunts. *It's well suited for her wide hips and protruding belly*, I thought.

"God, Dad," Jessica snapped. "Why do you always have to stop?"

"Ten minutes, Jessica," I said with an appeasing tone. "Ten minutes, and we blow the pop stand" As I walked toward the truck with my crowbar, I noticed the out-of-shape woman coming to me.

"My husband is a good provider, but he is not good with his hands." She touted with a scent of disapproval. "Just not a fixer-up type of guy."

I walked up to the bread truck. I noticed him gazing with frustration.

"Can I be of some help?" I said with politeness in my voice.

"I am having a difficult time opening this door," said the man.

Within a few minutes, we had the door open. Inside the truck there were shelves full of wrapped bread, pastries, and bagels. It was still April, and the nights had been pretty cool.

The contents seemed fresh. We took several loaves each.

The slight man spoke with a meek tone, "My name is Anthony. That's my wife. She doesn't think I am manly enough." He tried to hide a tear in his eye and tilted his gaze downward as his voice faded. "She started to gaze at other men."

I interrupted firmly to take attention away from his downward demeanor. "Look, you took action to find food. To me, that is a good man."

After I had gathered enough bread to meet our short-term needs, I walked out and went by the out-of-shape woman. She had undone a few of her top buttons in an attempt to attract my attention.

"That's a fine car, sir. Can you help us?" she exclaimed, trying to act sultry. "I could be very appreciative."

These are desperate times, I thought. *It's just human nature to try to survive.* Still, her attitude got under my skin, and I replied in a resonate tone, "You got a good man there. Many women would be happy to trade places with you."

We fit several loaves of bread in the trunk before I asked the girls to pack the rest under and around their feet. Fortunately Jessica didn't take up much room. She was a diet-conscious girl of medium height. However, Vivian was almost six feet tall, and she was a picky eater. So her attractive figure and large frame did not hinder our need to hide the loaves of bread. With the car now packed with spoils, I opened the door and entered with a smile. Both girls were really packed in. Neither complained. In fact, they both behaved like troopers. I started up our lifeline car and headed on toward our home base.

Once we were out of sight of the sultry woman, Jessica started the conversation with a firm voice and a noticeable frown. "That woman was a cheap hussy."

Perhaps it was guilt over my own behavior, but I felt a strong desire to give the hussy a break. "It's a survival mechanism in these troubled times," I retorted in a defensive way. "She is frustrated with her predicament on several levels."

"Mr. Randal?" Vivian asked in a puzzled voice.

"Yes, Vivian," I said.

"How did you know so quickly that it was an EMP nuke?"

"Well, Vivian," I replied in a fatherly voice. "The Mass Pike is really an encyclopedia. You see, Boston is a unique city. Many see it simply as the liberal bastion of the East with famous schools and hospitals. Being from Nebraska, I was in awe of the colleges. But I also recognized the research labs, high-tech companies, bio tech firms, and think tanks."

"You mean that many use the Mass Pike to get there," Vivian said, interrupting my moment in the spotlight.

"Yes, Vivian. Hundreds, probably thousands each day," I said like a male gorilla pounding his chest. "I was less than three miles from work when it hit. It was like watching the *Matrix* when it went into a pause. Damn, I thought my new Honda Accord was failing on me. I tried turning the key several times before I started to figure this out. After a few stunned minutes, I surveyed my surroundings. Holy crap. All the vehicles on the Mass Pike were in the same predicament. Could this be a UFO? Maybe a government test? How about some kind of solar or comet disruption? I was really perplexed.

"None of this made sense. I looked up, searching for an alien ship. Maybe they'll do a reset, you know. Like when you shake an Etch A Sketch to clean up a messy picture. Nope, this is the new reality. I reached in my glove compartment and took out my vehicle registration. As I opened my car door to get a better view, I saw hundreds of disabled cars. *What's the point?* I thought. It was like the blizzard of '78 just without the snow. Who cares about ownership right now? I turned around and put my registration back in my glove department.

"It was a little cool, but it was a good day for a walk. With my bottle of water, I started my own walk. *The curse of the Boston Marathon*, I thought and frowned. Unless this problem was quickly resolved, there was no way the Boston Marathon could be held in less than a week. In Boston, the curse of the Bambino was infamous. The owner of the Red Sox traded away Babe Ruth to the dreaded New York Yankees for a pittance. The Sox then went on to an eighty-year drought without winning the World Series.

"The Sox usually started with all guns blazing. Shortly after Memorial Day, it was like a gunner shot out the plane's rudder. The plane slowly descends and then falls downward to its demise. The cry in Boston was, 'Wait until Next Year.' The problem was that the curse just didn't quit. They finally beat the impenetrable Darth Vader. Now it seems the Boston Marathon has its own mini curse. Many of the top runners are in Boston.

"It would have taken me all day to walk home. I wished I had sneakers on, but I would survive. I looked at my cell phone for the time. Old habits are hard to break. Nothing, just junk. God, one doesn't realize how much we depend on electronics."

"Well, Vivian," I continued with my monologue, "There were hundreds and hundreds of stranded cars. Some were angry, but most were in shock. In my work I have learned to block out the noise. Cursing resolves nothing. I always keep my eye on what is important.

"After a good twenty-minute walk, I approached a black Volvo. An older, out-of-shape man with white hair and a wrinkled tweed sports

MICHAEL KRAVITZ

coat stepped out of his car. He started to mumble some English with a foreign accent. He spoke as though I was not there.

"The man said, 'It has to be an EMP nuke explosion, but why? The Russians and Chinese know that there would be a counterattack. That North Korean dictator is a narcissistic brute, but he is not suicidal or stupid. That leaves only a few. Whoever it was has to be well financed. They are fanatical, idealistic, and not afraid for their own mortal well-being. I wish I had a survival radio.'

"'Excuse me,' I said. 'I have a survival radio.'"

"With his train of thought interrupted, he looked at me. 'What did you say?'"

"'I have a survival radio. I inherited it.'"

"'Lucky you,' He said in astonishment. 'I always listen to those off-beat videos on the Internet. I was a fan of *Info Wars* and several other survivalist theorists. Deep down I knew they were on to something. I just never followed up.'"

"Well, Vivian, I did speak with a number of others. Some were common working folks, but many spoke like professors, technical researchers, or other professionals. There was one common answer—an EMP nuke."

My story was over. The mystery was solved in Vivian's mind. Our trip so far had been an emotional roller coaster. Our vintage Buick was coming down to the last twenty miles. As I weaved around a minibus, a sickening feeling ran down my gut. On the right several hundred yards ahead, there was that Mustang we had seen earlier. This time the situation had intensified. The old woman was lying face down, motionless. There were more of those two-legged rats. Jessica was making small talk with me, but I could not concentrate on what she was saying.

My sweaty hands gripped the steering wheel tightly. I knew I had to drive right into the eye of this upcoming storm. Our survival and that of my wife and son dictated that I had to keep going. If I tried to speed up, I knew we would face a wall of gunfire. I kept going at a slow, deliberate rate. The old man was leaning up against his Mustang. He looked like a rag doll. They worked this defenseless man hard. Several hundred feet away, the angry woman turned toward us. I yelled, "Get your heads down, girls."

"What's wrong, Mr. Randal?" Vivian asked with a fearful voice.

"It's that yellow Mustang," I said with a calm voice. "It seems that the angry bitch has more rats following her flock."

She motioned to her leader as we got closer, and the old man started walking down the hill. The angry bitch followed with a handful of her flock. Within a hundred feet, I stopped the Buick at a forty-five-degree angle and slowly opened the door. With more deliberate attention, I stepped out even slower. I grabbed my rifle by its barrel and tucked it under my arm so no one could see it. All the time I kept looking at them, but mostly I looked at that angry bitch. She made me itchy. I leaned the rifle against the Buick with the stock up. They were now within seventy feet.

"What's happening, Dad?" Jessica asked with a cry in her voice.

"Be quiet. This will be over soon. Everything will be all right," I said in a deliberate command. I looked at the leader. He was a tall, sloppy, skinny creep. I yelled out an unmistakable command: "Stop right there!"

"Yo, pops!" the creep said, "that's a nice set of wheels you have. We're in the business of collecting nice wheels. Just walk away, and no one will get hurt." He gazed at all the water bottles.

"You mean like that old lady lying face down," I answered in a defiant manner.

"We're wasting our time with him," the angry bitch proclaimed.

"Shut up, you stupid bitch," the creep answered. "You shouldn't have killed that old lady."

"I couldn't take her mouth anymore," the angry bitch replied, increasing the anger in her voice.

"You're outnumbered. It's a losing position for you," the creep said.

"You lose," said the little runt, who was five feet behind the angry lady. He began stroking the 9mm gun in his right hand. The rest of the flock may have been along for the ride, but the creep, the angry bitch, and the runt had guns.

"Screw this," the creep muttered as he took a step closer.

"Oh, God, please," Vivian started to cry as she lay out of sight in the backseat.

At this moment my heart was beating so fast that I felt the pounding in my head. I knew this would not end well. And it wasn't going to last more than a few more fleeting seconds. With my right hand, I lifted the rifle by its barrel. At seventy-five feet, I felt I had the upper hand.

If they got within forty to fifty feet, they would have the advantage. I pointed the rifle at the creep's right shoulder, his shooting arm. I yelled even louder, "Stop! Turn around! And go away." He raised his gun in a threatening manner. Instinctively I squeezed the trigger. With a loud noise, the spent round hit its mark. Both Vivian and Jessica covered their ears and started screaming. The creep immediately flinched back with immediate shock. He let the grip lose on his gun, and it fell to the ground.

This infuriated the angry bitch. She pointed her hand gun at me and fired. The round came close to me and smashed into the side mirror. As the shattered pieces were flying about, I pivoted my rifle right at her. Out of immediate and total fear, I aimed my rifle at the middle of her body. I had to squeeze my trigger before she could. The surge of adrenaline in my system erased the feel of the trigger as I squeezed it in a flash of fear and anxiety.

The angry bitch fell backward. Like a movie, her heavy frame went backward in slow motion as her gun slipped from her fingers. Split seconds turned into an eternity. Instinctively I looked at the little runt. I knew I had to end it right here and right now … and hopefully with no more bloodshed. I lifted my rifle like a soldier in boot camp. I ran right for the runt. He scurried away like a bowlegged cartoon cowboy into the sunset. Without its head, the rest slithered away.

For a few seconds, I watched intently as the flock put distance between them and me. The deceased old lady and the lifeless angry bitch lay near each other. With trepidation I walked slowly toward them. The angry bitch was laid out on her back, motionless, her eyes wide open. Her face showed pain with a slight trail of blood running down the side of her mouth. In the upper part of her chest, I saw the bullet hole. It had penetrated through her leather jacket. With my right foot, I kicked the gun away. My two fingers on her throat found that her soul had departed the vessel. The two girls came running out of the Buick.

"Dad! Dad! You're alive!" Jessica yelled with a cry in her voice.

Less than five feet away from the angry bitch, I knelt down and started to heave. I put both hands on the ground and continued my ordeal. Both girls came over to me, crying and nervously laughing. Jessica put her arms around me. "Dad, I love you. It's all right. You had no choice. Please, Dad, you did what you had to do."

Vivian was next to us, but she was staring at the horizon, keeping a close watch for the rest of the flock. I collected myself, and with a slow, soft voice, I said, "Vivian, please take the keys out of the ignition."

"Yes, Mr. Randal," Vivian said.

I slowly got up and picked up my rifle. Jessica and I walked to the Mustang. The old man was in great pain. He spoke, but the words came out with a grimace. "My wife's dead. My wife. You can't leave her there. You see—" He started to cry. Then he continued, "The dogs ... the dogs are wild. They'll get at her."

At this point Vivian was coming with the keys in hand. "Vivian, please get that gun." I pointed with a nod of my head. "Would you mind checking her pockets ... for ammo clips?"

Vivian knelt down with a solemn look. With a face that showed total disgust, she put her right hand on the hip of the dead angry bitch. She had to roll her over to get to her back pocket. There were two clips.

"Yuck," she said as she walked away from the angry bitch. "I need to wash my hands."

"Okay," I said to Vivian. "Let's clean out the Mustang." After a few minutes, Jessica and I grabbed his wife. I took her upper body, and Jessica grabbed her legs. She was heavy. We put her down next to the door of the Mustang. I opened the door, and we had her halfway in. At this point Jessica let me handle her. I lifted her around the waist and gently put her in backseat.

"Okay, Jessica, let's get the other." She followed me, and I grabbed the corpse of angry bitch under her torso. Jessica grabbed her kegs. Vivian was happy not to be part of it.

"Stop," yelled the old man. "That bitch killed my wife. Not in my car with my wife."

I did not want to argue. Time was wasting. Jessica and I bought her to another car nearby. I broke the window and opened the door. With as much respect to her corpse as we could muster, Jessica and I gently put her in the backseat.

The runt and the others viewed from a distance. I told the old man, "Grab your keys." He did. He started to lock the car. I said, "Stop. If those degenerates want in your car, they will break the window." He knew I was right. "Look," I said. "How far to the nearest hospital."

"Not far. Less than ten minutes," the old man replied in pain.

I hated to do this, but he sat in the front passenger seat. Jessica had to sit on his lap since she weighed the least. I took a few more bottles of water and bread out from around him and stored some in the trunk and the others with Vivian. Poor girl, she almost needed a periscope to see out beyond the pile. We soon pulled off 95 and into Providence.

"The hospital is just two streets away," the old man said with even more pain.

As we were turning the corner, there were two city policemen on bikes.

"Stop," said the nearest one. I turned my car around and drove away. We turned down the hill. I stopped. I said to the old man, "I'm sorry. This is as far as we go. The cops want our car." Jessica opened the door and let him out. I disassembled the periscope and rearranged the stuff around Vivian.

"Thanks," the old man said with even more pain. "I don't care anymore. My wife was my whole life. How can I go on? Why should I go on?"

"Bye," Jessica said with a meek voice.

Soon we were back on 95. Thankfully there were no more dramatic incidents. It had been the most defining day of my life. I didn't need any more drama, especially not right now.

CHAPTER 3

Collaborative

A S WE ENTERED Massachusetts on I-95, we sighed with relief. It had been an emotionally and physically draining day. The last fifteen minutes was filled with silence, not the stoic kind but the kind that admits the limitations words. Vivian was spacing out, twirling her hair. Jessica looked out the window like a sad, lost puppy. I was lost in my head, drifting from moment to moment of happier times before all this EMP shit began. I couldn't allow thoughts of those last seconds before I squeezed the trigger at the angry bitch to surface. The repetitive recriminations of what-if thinking would doom us right now. We had to breathe in some relief first. Survival demanded it that away.

"Hey, Dad," Jessica shouted. "You're going past the exit."

Whoa! I thought. *What I am doing?* "Thanks, Jessica," I replied as I returned to the present. I stopped, backed up the car, and proceeded to our exit.

Most of the same cars were still stranded on the road. A few were pushed to the side, including the SUV with broken windows. Even in the affluent neighborhoods, there were some really bad apples. As we were anticipating our arrival, we passed the attorney Schiller's house. He owned a corporate law firm in downtown Boston. His home was a monstrosity of a palace, gated with at least one and a half acres of manicured lawn. My guess was that his BMW had met the same fate as mine. I wondered if his security systems still worked.

The last three years in the Boston area, we have had very cold and snowy winters. During a three-day nor'easter, it was common to lose electricity in the suburbs. It was very costly to purchase a natural gas generator and have it wired in if you were fortunate to have natural gas on your street. Unlike oil, there are no delivery trucks, and there is a meter that registers usage, which is all very convenient. The Schiller's have an automatic natural gas generator. As long as the gas keeps coming, he will have electricity. The main problem though was that their home would make for a well-lit target.

We were now within minutes of our home. When our neighbors heard our car, they started coming outside. Its distinctive noise was the sound of a lifeline. "Crap," I said out loud. "Too much notoriety." It was difficult to stay under the radar when you were the only game in town. We drove by Officer Ryan's house. His straight three-bedroom ranch had a small but well-maintained lawn. It represented the two-mile mark from our home. He had both his car and the blue and tan squad car in the driveway. He was on the night shift. He was a Massachusetts State Trooper.

All the time I lived here, he never talked much to me or his neighbors. Maybe he thought it would be a conflict of interest. Or perhaps it meant he wanted to maintain a professional distance. But this time he did a half salute with two fingers while he was dressed in blue jeans and his trooper's tee shirt. I was sure to wave back. There was no use in burning that bridge.

"Hmm, girls, that was weird," I muttered softly. I imagined him like my drill sergeant in basic training. It was the army way or no way. There was no deviation, no adaptation. When we fought the red coats, did we not adapt? Were they not lined up in a row and the patriots fired from behind trees and stone walls? Maybe I misjudged him.

As we pulled in the yard, both Alice and Randy heard the Buick's engine. Without a TV, cell phone, radio, or other electronic gadgets, one picks up an engine sound very quickly. Our house was a twenty-year-old colonial. It sat on a little more than an acre of land. A nice work shed sat in the back of the house. Randy and I spent a lot of time there working on the Buick, the lawn mower, and the snow blower. The land sloped in the back to a swampy, wooded area. The realtor had showed this feature last. Somehow she knew our wants and needs, making sure to satisfy them first.

Alice hugged both Jessica and me. Randy had a big smile and was about to say something. "What the f--- happen to my mirror?" Randy exclaimed in shock.

"We went through a lot, didn't we, Dad?" said Jessica.

"Yes, Jessica. Yes, we did," I replied, about to collapse.

"Hi, honey," Vivian's mom said to her daughter. Vivian's mom was shorter than her daughter. She also had a full figure. She wore a light black jacket, dress jeans, and a pullover blouse. It was not a typical biker's outfit.

"Mom, how did you get here?"

"Your cousin's bike. God, am I out of shape," Vivian's mom touted.

Before I could tell Randy what to do, he grabbed the keys and pulled the car behind the shed so it was out of sight from the road.

Everyone chipped in to carry in the water, bread, and corn. As we walked into the house, Alice informed me that it had been a stressful day for her and Randy too. I didn't even get a chance to unwind or talk about the day's event. I went to the bathroom to wash my face and brush my teeth.

No hot water gets old very fast. But we did have a gas stove. So far there was still gas coming through the town pipes. The main problem was that there was no electrical ignition. We had to turn on the knob and use a lighter. So far most of us just take GI baths.

Today's events started to annoy Alice. She informed me that the police chief came by twice to talk about the Buick. "I think they wanted to confiscate it," she said.

Vivian's mom was in the kitchen. To me, this was not a good time to air out family laundry.

"Ben," Alice commented with anger and frustration.

"Yes, dear," I calmly replied, wishing I could just have a nightcap to calm my nerves.

"There has been a steady stream of neighbors and strangers coming here today," she said with a determined point of view. "It seems many people know of our survival radio … and the Buick." In a despondent voice, she continued, "Some had the audacity to ask to use our stove to cook on. These are people I have never seen before."

"Dad," Randy now chimed in.

"Yes, son," I said as if I had the option to ignore him.

"Mom and I listen to the radio," Randy said. "It seems that not only the president but also the governor has declared martial law for our state."

I slowly looked at Vivian and her mom. I knew there could not be a reasonable conclusion. I was really emotional and beaten up. "Today I took someone's life. I am not myself," I said, but Alice pushed on.

"Look, Ben, Randy and I have been considering that we need to act," she said with a commanding voice.

"Not tonight please. We will have a family meeting in the morning."

With angry and deep emotion, Alice shouted, "I am the one who worked, cooked, and took care of the kids. I am due my respect." Then she started to cry.

"Yeah, Dad," Randy said. "We have the car. We have marketing talents. We can go north."

"What makes you the boss? It's my car. I paid for it. I repaired it." Randy left and slammed the bedroom door. Anger and frustration was showing their ugly heads. Vivian's mom walked over to me. She was wearing a large cross on her neck.

"Mr. Randal, sir," she said in a soothing tenure.

"Yes," I replied, hoping that this was not going to be a lecture.

She reached in her coat pocket and pulled out a small Bible. "Mr. Randal, you've been a good influence on my daughter. You have been a father figure to her. This has had a stabilizing effect on her and me. I came here today and kept my hand on this Bible. I prayed. Dear Jesus, please keep the Devil away. Tonight, Mr. Randal, I want you to hold this Bible to make you strong. I pray for you to have the courage to do the right thing." She smiled.

"Thank you," I said.

"Vivian and I will leave now. We've got an hour of sunlight left."

"No, you can't. Please not now. There is some water and bread for you. Two women walking alone without a cell phone or protection is not safe. One dead woman is all I can live with. I will calmly make a concession to my wife tonight," I said with resignation. "I will agree to the move in two days. I know we can survive this. The house and money are material things. God and my family are important. Even if in my heart I feel that it is the wrong move, I will do it," I said with a slow, sad, and soft tone. I continued, "You have given me strength. Tonight please sleep on my sofa and loveseat. Tomorrow morning there will be no drama. Randy has a car and .22 rifle. You'll be safe."

"Mr. Randal," Vivian said, twirling her hair.

"Yes, Vivian," I replied.

"I still have the gun, you know, from the angry bitch," Vivian stated, showing it to me.

"You're right, Vivian," I stated, my mind going into overdrive.

Jessica heard her mom crying. She made a vain attempt to communicate.

"Not now, Jessica," her mother replied as Jessica tapped at her bedroom door.

I saw to it that Vivian and her mom were all set. The temperature this April night was in the upper forties. I gave each of them a quilt and one towel. I had to shampoo my hair in cold water. I put on a bathrobe and clean underwear.

God, this is going to be difficult, I thought. It had been an hour since all of the drama. I held the little Bible tight. I slowly opened the door. My wife was sleeping on her side, facing away from me.

That was uncharacteristic. "All right, honey, we will leave. All I beg for is two days. Today Jessica and I went through a lot. I took a woman's life. I need to digest everything. It is difficult not only for us but for the whole country," I commented as I pulled the blanket over me.

Alice put her hand on her mouth. I know she wanted to hug me. It was her own fleeting ego that stopped her. Both of us were emotionally drained. I slept with a tight grip on my borrowed Bible. Somehow it gave me a second wind.

Morning came. Days were getting longer, but it was still a chilly morning. Vivian and her mom were up. It's hard to sleep when you're not in your own element.

I looked at both as I headed to the bathroom.

"Morning, ladies," I said, trying to sound cheery.

"Morning, Mr. Randall," they said almost in unison.

After I finished with the bathroom, I went to Vivian's mom, kissed the Bible, and handed back to her. I spoke clearly to both. "The pain is real. I have to come to terms with it."

As I was walking away, Vivian's mom stated slowly and clearly, "God has his own way and his own timetable. He will lift your grief."

"I pray so. I pray so," I said as I continued walking away.

Alice got up. "Well, the milk will go sour soon. We also have a couple dozen eggs," she said with an accommodating voice.

"The French toast was not bad. I never got used to instant coffee, but it's better than no coffee," Randy blurted in his pissy mood, while Jessica joined us at the table.

"Randy," I said, "we will leave in two days." I had to throw him a bone to stroke his ego. "Would you be so kind as to drive Vivian and her mom home?" I said with empathy.

Feeling a little embarrassed and guilty, Randy replied, "Sure, Dad."

Vivian and her mom grab some water and bread. As they were leaving, I said, "Son."

"Yes, Dad," Randy replied.

"Grab your .22 rifle and a few clips," I said with calmness. "Come right back."

They got into the Buick and left. Alice and I did not talk much that morning. I did not want to listen to the survival radio. Somehow I knew it would make matters worse.

"Alice, I am going for a short walk. I'll be back soon," I tried to say with respect.

"All right" she replied indifferently without bothering to look up.

The cold war between us was still on. *Gads*, I thought, *I'm in a no-win situation.* So I decided to go off to see my friend William, who lived down the street behind a gated driveway. He always had a calming effect when there was a storm.

Since it was harder now to keep clothes clean, I put on my gray sweatshirt and wore the same blue jeans as yesterday. It was a quiet street with a half dozen homes. I couldn't ring the buzzer because there was no electricity. Fred was outside.

William's wife signed up to provide care services for Fred. He was a challenged man in his seventies. Age had shrunk his height by a few inches. He stood close to five-foot-seven. He was a compulsive eater. The state of Massachusetts was a leader when it came to the care of the challenged. Fred had a low IQ and was now a ward of the state. He had only a few teeth and was mostly bald. Usually he was smiling.

Every day he poured birdseed into the feeder, but today he was cursing the squirrels. He was totally oblivious to what had happen, and now he was putting up a sign. Since he couldn't write, he would scribble. "Hi, Mr. Randal. Just feeding the birds. I'm mad today the squirrels are stealing their food. I am writing a sign on a sheet of copier paper. It says, 'no squirrels allowed.'"

"Would you mind telling William that I would like to talk to him?" I said with respect.

"I will. Something is wrong with my TV. I can't turn it on, and the van never came today," Fred said while he was in his own world.

I met William four years ago while trying to do a little exercise during the week. As I biked past his house, he said hello. His wife, Ruby, was a teacher nearby. Like Fred, Ruby also liked to eat beyond normal limits. My wife found her a little overpowering, very quick with opinions, and a little short on sensitivity.

William was the polar opposite. At six-foot-one, his body only carried 170 pounds. I never saw him drink alcohol or eat meat. He was a very picky eater. He explained that he played Ping-Pong at the community center two to three times a week. He offered to take me if I was interested. I told him that while I was in the army, I played Ping-Pong. We were often on call, confined to the base, so I'd spend all my free time in the day room. There were several paddles usually without rubber on them. We chipped in to buy white Ping-Pong balls. They were always on sale at the rec room. I learned to hit the ball hard and developed a good rhythm.

Being from the Midwest, Alice knew I was not a womanizer. She encouraged me to have outside activities. She was a homebody. Family, cooking, cleaning, and a few sitcoms made her content. For me, I had to get away a little. I did like to go to the casino. It was a break from reality. There were no clocks, no pretense. It was another dimension of therapeutic escape. It beats paying the high price for a therapist. Plus I can have all the free drinks I want. To be honest, I was basically a social drinker. Foxwoods is a classy place. The drinks were watered down. They did not want a bad reputation. If I took a trip to Atlantic City, it was a different story. Two or three drinks, and I need an aspirin.

As I got older, I had to be pragmatic about exercise. Golf's a lovely game. It is time-consuming, expensive, and not really me. Tennis is a great game. In the Boston area, you should start looking to play inside starting in late October. Another big activity is darts.

It is a real fad. The throw line is three to four inches shorter than it is in England. Many of the bars support local teams. It's great for business. Lifting a Bud is the only exercise. The calories that one gobbles down will cause a floatation device around a midsection.

William was right. Your mind and body needed to be tuned. With great anticipation I went with him to a Ping-Pong game. He was gracious enough to lend me a paddle. The rubber was different on each side. One was a little softer than the other. He explained that one was for control and that the other was for speed. Control? What was he talking about? I just wanted to hit it and deliver a Roger Clemens fastball. As I entered the center, I was amazed by the exquisite community center. The playroom had a pool table, shuffleboard, and a Ping-Pong table. There were leather chairs and a leather sofa. This was a high-end center.

We rallied for a good twenty minutes. He played to my level. Soon five Chinese players entered the room. They came mostly on a senior bus. Some who lived nearby did bike. William was a giving person. He invited them for a game of doubles. Ping-Pong was usually a game of singles, and you played until you reached eleven. We were the geriatric group. Most were senior citizens. They played doubles. It was less taxing. We also played to twenty-one. Still it was like tennis. You had to win by two.

William and I rallied with two Chinese players. Their Ping-Pong paddles were different. They had a shorter handle. They gripped the racquet with four fingers spread out and their thumbs in.

I grabbed mine like I did with a tennis racquet. We were ready. The game was afoot. *Shock and Awe,* that is how my first game went. The two Chinese players not only placed the Ping-Pong ball well but it came with a lot of spin. I really felt like a fool. My turn to serve. I hit a fast one just over the net. It did not bother them. They returned it with either an undercut or overcut to William. He handled it well. The problem was me. I could not handle it.

When it came my turn to receive, it was soon apparent that I wasn't as skilled. The Chinese players I met were older and slender. Most were short, although a few were more than six foot.

This was their pastime. There were tables in homes throughout China. They learned to play right after they learned to walk. The lady could not speak English. She served an undercut spin. I blocked the shot, and it went into the net. The last two were overcut, and I nearly returned the shot to the ceiling. The Chinese player laughed. At first I thought it was an insult. Later I found that it is custom to laugh off your mistakes. They did it to themselves. In an hour or two, one can get a lot of exercise. Afterward, I would sit and talk with William. He was extremely intellectual.

There was a good mix of American, Chinese, and a few Russian players. Most of us were older.

After several weeks I noticed a lot of the Chinese players (not all) would only play with or against me for a short while. My level of play was likely not enticing. William suggested I take a few lessons. I talked to Alice. She asked if I enjoyed the game and the people. I told her, "I really look forward to it. The social interaction and exercise suit me."

She said, "Go for it."

William and I went to a town near Boston. They rented out a gymnasium. The master who ran the show was a high-seated player. There were six tables and buffers around all of them.

There were several Chinese players. It was different. They were mostly young and training for tournaments. There were also several white players. Most of them came from Cambridge.

God, what a culture shock. It was east meets west. The city of Boston is known for its liberal political leanings, but Cambridge went to the extreme. Folks from outside of the greater Boston area often joke that the Cambridge city limit signs should read: "Entering the People's Republic of Cambridge." The players from Cambridge were white and very serious players. Most looked like they were ready for a GI inspection. Their shorts, socks, sneakers, and racquets were all pristine.

I felt a little intimidated. William was there, and he brought Fred with him. Fred did like to go. He picked up the Ping-Pong balls and handed them to everyone. He really felt accepted. With reluctance, I signed up both for play and lessons. The master's wife handled the sign-ups. She made me feel comfortable. "Don't worry," she exclaimed. "I will pair you up with another beginner."

Two hours went by. Then it was lesson time. I went to the table with the master. He spoke perfect English. He had a crate of four hundred Ping-Pong balls. We rallied for two minutes. He assessed my level immediately. In a diplomatic way, he commented that I had to relearn my technique.

I was told to go on the corner of the table and get in a crouching position. I had to make my hand and racquet function as one. He spat out Ping-Pong balls like a machine gun. As I returned one ball, another was already on its way. Backhand and then forehand. Over and over. The last ten minutes he served with underspin and over spin shots. He instructed me to mimic the server. If it was an underspin, I was to follow through with an underspin return.

Eureka. It really worked. My level of play was climbing. I came back for several weeks.

At this point I could play even some of the Cambridge players. Most were nice. One, however, had an elitist attitude. He had a beard and an unruly hairdo. I heard that he was a software engineer. He was a wannabe, so I challenged him. God, his serve had more of a loop than a Bill Lee slow curve pitch. I was humbled by a game that ended eleven to two. I thanked him. He walked away without a thank-you or a gesture.

William witnessed the whole event. He challenged the bearded player. Like a pool shark, He rallied just enough to keep up with him. The bearded one wanted to move on and said, "Let's play." William showed his pearly whites. His intensity and agility were high. He never allowed the bearded man to even score a point. He was humiliated.

This Sunday I felt would be my last lesson. I was becoming more accepted. A middle-aged Chinese man with two little boys came to me. He asked if I would like a game. Of course, I said yes. If my ego got any bigger, it would have consumed the whole building. "Great," he said. "My son wants to play a game." I looked down at the little tykes. *Gad, maybe they need a milk crate to stand on*, I thought. Their heads barely made it to the top of the table. I hesitated. Then I thought, *I cannot humiliate him as I was humiliated*. I accepted.

We rallied for a few minutes. That little tyke could play. I thought I would go easy on him. The first two points went to me. Then it was his turn to serve. He went to the corner of the table. He measured his distance so that it would be a legal serve. He held his racquet to the side. *What is he doing?* I asked myself. When he served, the spin on the ball took it to the side of the table. I did not even get my racquet on it. How much more humble pie could one eat? The score was ten to nine. One more point, and the little one was sending me to a therapist. He looked at his dad.

The dad gave him a signal with his hands. The little one acknowledged him.

The next three points went to me. I knew it was not me. The father was giving a lesson both to his son and one to me.

I went to him with my hands clasped and said, "Thank you for the game and your lesson." He smiled at me and put his hand on his son. He spoke to his son in Chinese, and the son answered in Chinese. I guessed he was saying, "Dad, you should have let me wipe that white dude out." I smiled and left the building.

Practice, more humiliation, and more practice have improved my game greatly. Now when I play at the community center, William observes something different. The people may be the same, but as Ed Sullivan said, "Showtime." My level of play now almost matches the Chinese players. To beat me, they have to play at their best. I had gained their respect. These were great memories of the past. Now the lights were out at the community center.

As I was speaking to Fred at William's house, I saw him come out the door. He opened the gate and invited me in. I walked with the bike to his porch. William was a good listener.

William had suffered two traumatic events in his life. The first happened when he was young. The other happened at his workplace in Boston. He had a high-level job with a major insurance company. In the end, the company did a personnel change, and William lost his job. It totally affected him. The unjust way they treated him did finally result in a large six-figure settlement. Money was never an issue with him. It was his fragile emotions that were severely damaged. He never spoke to me about his early childhood, and I never asked. Nor did I want to know. He did lend me a book he liked—Dr. Michael Newton's *Journey of Souls*. After I read it, I was even more impressed by William. The next time I met him I turned in his direction and said: "William, you're alright in my book. Someday I hope to be of kindred spirit."

I confided in him about the situation that happened between Alice and me. I said to him, "If I do not leave with her and Randy in two days, our marriage is over." William showed no emotion. After three to four minutes of silence, he muttered one word, "Collaborative."

I said, "What?"

William stated again, "A collaborative. You have water, bread, a Buick, and the survival radio. I have cases of peanut butter. Mr. Henderson is a contractor. He could dig a well for water. The Leonards' have a gas generator. You can use it at each house to run everyone's refrigerator. This way it keeps everyone food without spoiling. The Arnolds have always grown and used their own veggies."

I reiterated, "A collaborative. Hmm, William I am going to see Officer Ryan."

"Officer Ryan? He is two miles away. What does he bring to the mix?" asked William

"You remember the New Jersey mobster actor who died in Italy of a heart attack?"

"Yes, Ben, I remembered him," William answered with curiosity.

"Well, the mob boss always goes to one who is paying for protection," I said as a light went off in my head. Remember what the mob boss would say?

"Heh piss on you. Do right and no one bothers you. Then you don't need my protection." "We should do it right and invite Officer Ryan in I said turning to William. Please tell the neighbors there is a meeting at my house in two hours." I went home, got the bicycle, and explained my little game plan to Jessica. I told her to bring some spring water, two loaves of bread, and my one bottle of whiskey.

"Dad, are you inviting the man next door. He is a drunk," she stated in a sarcastic tone.

"Yes, him too, Jessica. If we don't, there will be hell to pay. I will be back," I said as I got on the bike and rode off to Officer Ryan's house. As I was peddling, I got a little nervous. I had never spoken to him. Two miles was easy on a bike.

"Officer Ryan, may I have just five minutes of your time?" I asked with confidence.

"We are all trying to survive this horrible event. My neighbors and I are forming a collaborative for our survival. I think we can help each other," I explained slowly.

"I am not sure." His arms were folded as a defensive gesture.

I continued," It would be for your benefit too. Wear at least part of your uniform and wear your gun. Each of us has something to contribute. Together we can survive. If we go it alone, it will be to our demise." I was finished. Saying anything else would be an effort in diminishing returns. I just got on my bike and left. After a short two-mile bike ride, I was home. My next-door neighbor, the drunk, was in my yard.

"How are you doing?" the old drunk said. He was thin, and his face showed the poison that heavy alcoholics drank. It was morning, so he was sober. He had lost his wife to cancer. His one daughter never talked to him. At least he was quite wealthy. "Your daughter talked to me," he continued. "I don't remember ever talking to her. She is a sweet little thing," he said with surprised. "I guess we are having a neighborhood meeting, and I am invited!" Then he wiped his nose. "No one ever cares about me. My large inheritance can't bring her back. This electricity thing does not bother me as much as the rest of you," he said with a whimper. "I am not hurting anyone with my drinking. I am waiting for the Lord to take me so I can join my wife," he exclaimed as he wiped a tear from his eyes.

Damn, I thought. I never knew this about him. "Do you still have that old watch? The one that John Cameron Swazi said, 'It just keeps on ticking.'"

"Of course I do." Then he showed to me. "This is a classic. It winds up with your hand. My wife and I saw the ad on TV. We watched *I Love Lucy*, and the *Ed Sullivan Show*. We would cuddle on the sofa. I always looked at the watch to see what time it was."

"Couldn't miss Ed or Lucy," he said with a smile.

"Please follow me," I asked kindly. I put and iron pipe in the ground. I then drew a circle around it. Next I put twelve rocks in equal distance. I then replaced two with larger rocks. I made sure they were opposite each other. I turned to our drunk and asked, "What time is it?"

"It's 10:35, time for my first drink," he replied as he looked at his watch.

I set the stones so that we had a sundial. The shadow now indicated the time.

"You really should eat a little before drinking," I said with a helpful voice.

"The elderly council says the same thing to me," he espoused. "They bring food over, but it spoiled in the fridge. Now they keep bringing canned food over. I have cases of food in the spare bedroom," he said like it was a problem to him.

"We are having a collaborative meeting here in one hour," I commented. "If you can hold off drinking until then, it would be an honor to have you attend." I was trying not to insult him. My mind clicked fast. "In little more than an hour, we all can take one little sip of whiskey." He looked at his watch again.

"We have a deal, I can wait another hour before I drink," the drunk replied.

Jessica came out as I had asked her. She bought the bread, water, and whiskey. I told Alice I was having the neighbors over for a meeting. She was not impressed. Most came within an hour. With no radio, TV, or electronic devices, entertainment was hard to come by. William brought the peanut butter. I had to adapt. *Too many to bring inside*, I thought. The cold war between Alice and I was still ongoing.

We scrounged up chairs, milk cartons, logs, coolers, tool chests, whatever it took to find seating. Almost everyone came. I first gave out water and a little food. I even insisted that the drunk have a peanut butter sandwich. He ate. I knew that when a despot feeds his followers, it becomes easier to lead them. I am not a natural leader, but instinct told me that I needed to gain their trust and respect. I bought a bunch of branches and left them at my feet. First I gave everyone a sip of whiskey. Only Jessica and, of course, William did not partake. The sundial indicated it was not even twelve noon. Randy looked. He shook his head, thinking, *Dad is drinking. Why not head to Canada with Mom now?*

I stood up. "Look, everyone, I am not much of a leader or speaker." I took a twig and broke it. But then I took a whole bunch and tried to break them. I showed everyone that I could not break them. "Maybe to most of you this is lame," I continued. "Truth is that we are in a bad situation. By ourselves we are doomed. Yesterday I went on a trip to get spring water. To defend my daughter and her friend, I had to shoot at two people. I took the life of a young woman. It really is out of my character. The rest of us may encounter the same crisis. Either we will hurt someone or be hurt."

I had everyone's attention. I continued, "Each of us has something to offer. My son has the Buick. I have the survival radio. The Henderson's can dig a well. They can dig it right over there." I pointed to a spot where the ground sloped down. "One has a gas generator. One has canned vegetables."

The drunk interrupted with a smile and said, "Besides a lot of alcohol, I also have a lot of canned food."

"A collaborative is pool of talent and resources. I want to survive like the rest of you," I said.

Ruby, William's wife, interrupted. "But your wife wants you to move to Canada in two days?" Most everyone turned to look at Alice. She turned and walked inside the house.

"Look, that is a possibility. We are working on it as a family. A good collaborative can survive with people coming or leaving."

"I'm bored," Mr. Henderson said. "My two sons and I are going to start digging. We will have you a well in a few hours."

"I will bring a few cases of canned food," the drunk replied.

Another offered to cook, and another to bring her veggies. Alice was still guarding our front door from our new friends. I thought it better to build a fire outside for cooking. My God, the collaborative was up and running. "Look, Randy, just tonight, please take the Buick out to the highway and look for delivery trucks." Randy seemed unsure of this new activity, so I said, "Fine, I will do it."

"Look, Mr. Randal, I am good at getting doors opened," one of Mr. Henderson's sons said. He was a brute of a man who weighed more than two hundred pounds and was all muscle.

"You will need protection," someone said. Everyone turned around. Damn, it was Officer Ryan.

Mr. Henderson's son got a couple of sledgehammers and crowbars. Randy started up the Buick. Mr. Henderson's son graciously offered Officer Ryan the front passenger seat.

Officer Ryan climbed in and asked Randy to stop at his house. Randy obliged. Officer Ryan came out with his uniform on. "Now you have an official Mass trooper to protect you."

Gads, it had been days since Randy had smiled. With adequate protection in place, they went off on their mission.

At the home front, digging the well proceeded smoothly. They didn't encounter any large rocks or heavy clay. Twelve feet down they hit water. Mr. Henderson was very clever. Out of a few birch trees he built a high horse over the well. This would act as a lowering mechanism to bring water up. We started the generator up. Each house got an hour of use from the generator. This way we could all keep food from spoiling. I was hoping if Randy came back in time, he could make another run for gasoline for the generator.

I had the fire going pretty high. With everyone chipping in, our survival camp was almost opened for business. I asked for a pool or tub. Mr. Henderson said he had a tub for cement mixing. Two of the neighbors had blow-up pools. It was slowly coming together. Randy came back then. They found an eighteen-wheeler. It still had food that had been scheduled for delivery to a large supermarket. The weather was still cool enough. Much of the produce was salvageable. Well water was generally safe to drink. But to be sure, we did what people in underdeveloped countries did. We boiled the water and then put it in a refrigerator.

Tonight I had to go for broke. I put a clothesline up. With old quilts hanging on the ropes, I relegated one area for washing and another for taking baths. A well and a good fire meant we had the means for heating water. With the generator running in the drunk's house, we hooked up a 220 line for his electric stove. One of the pools was for washing clothes and the other for warm baths. This reminded me of my days in Nebraska—the community getting together and bonding.

Dusk was nearing, and we had a roaring fire. Hot water was available both for washing and bathing. Everyone had chipped in. Now we drew names out of a hat to see who would get the bath first. At this point Alice came out of the house. She thought of our days in Nebraska too.

Sometimes the Almighty shows up in a mysterious way. The drunk said, "Let Mrs. Randal go first. This is her land and her husband's initiative."

"Yes, Mom, you first" Jessica said. She put her hand in the pool. It was warm. With the roaring fire, the whole atmosphere was tantalizing. Alice stepped behind the quilt and undressed.

She yelled out to Ben, "This doesn't change anything," As she tiptoed into the pool, a smile appeared on her face. "Oh, Jesus," she muttered softly. "This is heaven."

The old drunk was really shocking me. He whispered something to Jessica. The next thing I knew, Jessica said to her mother, "Mom, can I give you this?" With her head turned, she handed her mom a glass of White Zinfandel wine.

The stage was set. A seed was planted. As she toweled off, we drained the old water out and put new water in for the next person. Mr. Henderson had led a hose so that we could drain the water away from our area.

It was a grand night. We had food, wine, and clean clothes, and now we started to sing Neil Diamond songs. We sang as we held hands.

Then half of us repeated, "So good, so good, so good." It was the song that was always played at the Red Sox games. It was also a song we could sing with our limited musical talent.

Now it was getting late, and it was time for bed. I said to Alice, "I'm off to count sheep. I love you, Alice. I will keep my word. We can still leave in a day and half."

Alice had a half smile. It was a smile just the same. She exclaimed, "We'll see. We'll see. Good night." *Even in a Greek tragedy*, I thought, *there is always a moment of hope.* This was that moment. I had played out my hand. Now I need to let the dice roll.

That night, even though I went to sleep late, I slept well. It was warm near the fire. I just threw a few quilts over me as I breathed in the crisp, cool air. There was a saying in these parts. "If you do not like the weather, wait another day." Marathon day can come with hot weather or cool weather with rain and sleet. Usually when we have a cold, snowy winter, we have little or no spring. We jump straight into the hot weather. There was no electricity and no fan now. We were adapting.

I have learned to keep a pair of cotton PJs near me. Getting out of a warm bed into the crisp air is a bit like jumping into cold water. I put my PJs on under the covers. After a trip to the bathroom, it was time to get a little instant coffee. This time I put clean duds on. Today we would get the generator for thirty-five minutes. By using a power strip, there was a lot we could do. The freezer could make ice and keep the food from spoiling. I was sure Alice would be at the ironing board. I would also use the dryer to get the wrinkles out. Last night I had had too much to eat. Today I just needed my morning cup of caffeine.

As I opened the door, I found that the smell of the fire was still present. There was still a small flame where we were at. William and the drunk kept the place tidy. *What an odd alliance*, I thought. Now there was another small problem—rubbish. I figured I could throw everything that was burnable in the fire pit. *We really should have another meeting. Maybe tomorrow morning. Too much familiarity can bring out nasty traits in all of us. Rubbish will definitely be a topic.* I sat on a cooler. I couldn't shake the thought of that woman I shot. This was strange. I really needed consolation from my wife. There seemed to be a gradual thawing in her. I wondered if it was this hard for Henry Kissinger when he had to deal with the Russians during the Cold War.

The sundial was working. The time was a little after 9:00 a.m. After twenty minutes or so, Mr. Henderson and one of his son's came over.

"Morning, Mr. Randal," Mr. Henderson said with an enthusiastic attitude.

"It's great wearing clean clothes," he said with a smile.

"Sure is," his son chimed in. "Wonderful idea of yours, Mr. Randall. I mean, forming this collaborative. You give all of us hope when there was none."

"Everyone contributed," I replied, trying to be a little humble. "Hold on," I said quickly. "I will bring out some instant coffee." I went in the house, took my Bic lighter, and lit the gas stove. After I heated the water, I went outside. To my surprise, the son came back with some real cream for our coffee.

"Here you are, Mr. Randal," Mr. Henderson's son said with an uplifting tone. He continued, "It is not Dunkin' or Starbucks, but it will do."

At that moment Jessica stepped outside. Her hair seemed a little strung out, but otherwise she looked great. "Morning, Dad," she said cheerfully. "Morning," she said again as she gestured toward Mr. Henderson and his son.

Both the dad and son gave greetings to Jessica. Jessica's insecurity and the fact that she didn't want to lead on Mr. Henderson's son showed.

"Honey," I said to Jessica. "Heat up some instant coffee for yourself. The Hendersons brought some real cream." I did not want to mention his son's name to her. If I did that, I know she would have declined. She came out and sat to the left of me on a milk cartoon. It was her way of sending a subliminal message that these were the boundaries.

"My sons and I would like to come by and do a little more work on the well," he said in a respectful manner. "We would only spend a few hours a day here."

Just as I was about to speak, Alice came outside with a cup of hot instant coffee.

"Morning, Jessica," she said and kissed her on the cheeks.

"Morning, Mom," Jessica retorted gleefully. "Morning," Alice said to the rest of us.

God, I thought, *do I have leprosy or some contagious disease? This is getting old.* I wished the mail service was still running. I would have liked to order a Howard Stern blow-up doll. I could start napping with it in the shed. Not saying anything, Randy just joined us. He did partake in the coffee hour. The little pleasures made life worth living. That cream was a big hit.

"Mr. Randall," Mr. Henderson commented in a deep voice. "I always saw those ads on the Internet—you know, for the survival kits.

I thought it was a joke. Now I guess the joke is on me," he said, shaking his head.

"The ones that sell for thirty-seven dollars or the upgrades for ninety-seven," I said. With everyone looking at me I continued, "Some of you may want to have a shelter in the ground. Can you imagine living in a tight place underground with your family? Sleep, eat, go to the bathroom—after a few days, what do you talk about? How do you know when it is safe to come up? What if a family member asks to open the latch and check it out?" Now everyone was really listening. "I open the latch, look east, look west, and then *poof*, another nuke goes off."

"Houston," I said. "There's a problem. I lower the latch and come down. My hair is standing straight. My face is orange except where the sunglasses were."

At this point there was a smile on everyone's face, even Alice's. I continued on with my satire. "And what if you hear people feet above you, except they're speaking Russian or Chinese or some foul language, saying, 'God is great.' At this point everyone is laughing, including Alice. Since I was on a roll, I continued, "Maybe the safe thing to do is put a mailbox next to your latch. One can open the latch to check the mailbox. If there are bills in it, you can come up. If you can't afford them, go back down," I said, laughing at myself. I then retorted, "With my luck, I will get a knock at the latch door. I will open it, and it'll be an IRS agent in a gray suit." Everyone knocked the IRS.

"The IRS would say in a threatening, businesslike manner, 'Mr. Randal, you have a large bill that needs to be addressed.'"

"'Sir,' I would respond. 'The check is in the mail. Problem is that it was incinerated along with the postman.'"

At this point I finished my coffee, and then Mr. Henderson stood up. "My son and I are going to start. Oh, and Mrs. Randal, it's your turn at 2:00 p.m. with the generator. You might want to get ready. You know, clothes, electric heater, and your refrigerator," Mr. Henderson said before he walked away with his son.

With her hands clasped over her face, Alice cried with joy.

Damn, I thought. *William, you are a genius. Collaborative.* I got up and grabbed a rake. I thought I would rake a little around our new survival area. After an hour of raking, I started to cut tree limbs and gather any wood I could.

"Dad," Randy finally spoke up.

"Yes, son," I answered with trepidation. I did not know if this was going to be a good-bye speech or a question.

"Some of the neighbors have given me several more gas cans. I think we might as well hit it now before it is too late," he said in a tone that was more of a question than a statement.

"Randy," I said firmly, "it is a good idea. Make sure you at least ask Officer Ryan."

Then I looked at him with a fatherly look. "No women with you. Make sure you have at least two or three for safety." Then I concluded my instructions to him in a stern, direct way.

"Yes, Pops," Randy replied with a very happy and respectful tone.

I continued on with the wood cutting while Jessica went inside with Alice.

"Mom," Jessica said to Alice.

"Yes, dear," Alice said sweetly. She was still in a joyful mood.

"I do not think you're being fair to Dad," Jessica said in a tone of disapproval. "Dad is a good provider, and he is really trying to hold us together. It's hard enough for him to protect and provide for us. He threw up and almost broke down when he shot that angry bitch." With a little anger at her mom, she continued, "I see his face every time you give him a short answer. It's not right."

"I think you're right, dear. I worked so hard when we were in Nebraska. I worked teaching all day. At night I had to cook, clean, go grocery shopping. Grad school was hard for your dad. It was his ticket for all of us to have a better life. I feel frustrated. I can see what your dad is doing to survive this," she said remorsefully. "Sometimes when you are older, you will have the motherly instincts. We feel more than we think. It is in our special nature to be motherly, protecting."

Enough said. Jessica left the kitchen area to gather some of her clothes. She wanted a few of the clean blouses ironed. When they come with the generator, Alice wanted thirty-five minutes of ironing.

After I finished with the wood cutting, I went for a short walk. The drunk and a few neighbors greeted me. They wanted to know when the next collaborative meeting would be held. I tried telling everyone that there wasn't any boss. But to be practical, I suggested a meeting the next day around 1:00 p.m. I explained that I had heard on the survival radio that the president would speak at 2:00 p.m. and that we needed to know as much as possible. Perhaps it was my down to earth upbringing in Nebraska, together with the hours of having to listening to my father in law, the survivalist. Folks started to get the feeling that I was the 'all wise protector'. On the inside however, I struggled. There was conflict between having some practical answers and understanding that I am not a leader who has to coddle his subjects. We all have something to contribute.

Strange, inside or outside our house, it was the same. No electronic devices, little heat. Today, with the generator, there would be some heat. Two people came with the generator. They placed it right outside the kitchen door. Alice and Jessica were waiting. Both seemed a little giddy. One man wheeled the generator around. It had its own wheels. The other had a wheelbarrow. It carried gasoline and a twenty-five-foot extension cord. After they checked the oil level, they pulled out the chord.

The noise was like listening to the Boston Pops. The house jumped with life. The refrigerator, the iron, and the electric heater were all in sync. *Home sweet home.*

William and Fred were walking down the road. William seemed more inclined to be in the company of Fred than his wife. With his age and weighing more than two hundred pounds, Fred fought a constant battle with diabetes. Fred's kidneys could no longer take the high dosage of diabetes pills. He had to have insulin needles two to three times a day. William was very methodical about Fred's care.

William had several months of insulin. He had chosen the viles instead of the pens. The syringes would run out in a few weeks. William was concerned with Fred's sugar levels. I had told William that I planned on a trip to Boston within two days. It had now been a good week since the EMP blast. News was sketchy, and the mood among the masses was becoming more desperate.

"Look, William," I said sincerely. "I have to go to the hospital to check on my mother-in-law. I will try to barter with the doctor. There has to be some basic medical supplies shipped in soon. The military planes have some protection with a built-in Faraday shield. We have to be positive."

"Thanks," he said with a downtrodden look. "I have not thrown the syringes away. If I have to, I will dip them in alcohol and reuse them. It is better than no insulin shots."

"There are a lot of hardships," I continued. "The government was slow to react when Katrina hit. They were also slow when the hurricane hit Atlantic City." With a disappointing mood, I continued, "I remember CNN and Fox reporting from the Superdome in New Orleans. A short bus ride could have bought them to a better environment. In all fairness, I don't know if it is a responsibility of the state or the federal government. I know the feds can't violate a state's law. What I do not get is the lack of communication," I said slowly and softly. "There were many who lived in inhuman conditions. There were also many who died. Atlantic City was also badly handled." William nodded in agreement.

"Tomorrow we will have a collaborative meeting," I said cheerfully. "The president will speak at 2:00 p.m. I feel he seems to really care about the people," I commented with optimism. I looked at Fred. "God, he still is happy. He does not know the realty of the situation. All he knows is that he is taken care of. His mind seems to be on his bird feeder and those pesky squirrels."

William headed back with Fred at a slow pace. I was sure his wife would feed Fred and William. It was a crapshoot to what I might find stepping inside my own home. Within fifty feet, I heard the Buick pull up. Randy seemed to have had a good outing. There were many stranded cars with gas in them.

"Look, Pops. The collaborative is well stocked with gasoline," he said.

"Great job," I said in a supporting tone. "That should really bring everyone's morale up when we meet tomorrow. I continued on to our door. Randy parked the Buick in the back.

Alice was cooking on the stove. "I guess its spaghetti night," I said to Jessica. She had this mischievous smile, a smile that told me something was about to happen. I went into the bedroom.

My clothes were not only cleaned but also pressed. There was a candle burning on the dresser. Outside it was still a bit chilly, typical April weather. Inside seemed warm. The electric heater was still a little warm, and the gas stove also was throwing some heat.

"What do you think, Dad? Nice to have clean, pressed clothes?" Jessica said with excitement. "Mom and I make a good team." Alice was trying to hide her smile.

Randy came in and immediately noticed the warmth and his pressed clothes. "Mom, it smells good. When are we going to eat?" Randy said cheerfully.

"In about one hour," she said softly. "Would you mind setting the plates?"

We sat down and had a great meal. Alice also bought a bottle of wine to the table. *This is a strange way of smoking the peace pipe*, I thought, but I was grateful to see the thaw in her face.

At the dinner table, Randy related his experiences on the highway. And he talked about some of the people who were looking for anything they can find. "It's a wasteland. Debris everywhere. I hate seeing the broken windows. There are some fine cars. The trucks we went into yesterday are now pretty empty. As we were driving, we could see smoke coming out of the strip mall by the highway," Randy said as he finished with his little salad. "Dad, I think we should check on Grandma soon."

Jesus, I thought. *Did we not just finish the cold war? Is this what therapy is? Are we to carry on like nothing happened?* I thought of opening up a dialogue, but maybe this had been stressful enough on all of us. I needed to think before I speak. I was still trying to figure out the woman's mind.

"I really appreciate a nice, warm meal," I said. I figured that was my way of smoking the peace pipe.

"Many of the runners would eat a big carb dinner the night before the marathon," Jessica chimed in. "Where they start the race is a long ways from the finish line."

"Over twenty-six miles," Randy boastfully said. Cars and sports were Randy forte. Now that dinner was over, I helped with the cleanup.

"It's nice to have a full belly and a warm home." I said trying to make small talk.

"Last night Ben reminded me of our days in Nebraska," Alice said in a romantic way. "I really enjoy the culture, malls, and the opportunities of the East Coast," she said. I could feel a big *but* coming. "There was more caring and gatherings of our neighbors back home," said Alice, taking a little trip down memory lane.

I felt like this was letting out the fish line. You have to feel it out. "Well, dear," I said, trying to accelerate the thawing, "tomorrow is our meeting. There is a lot to talk about it. I also feel like the collaborative is bonding well," I commented, choosing my words carefully. "The next day we can leave for Boston."

In a deliberate way, I stated, "Tomorrow the president is going to speak. I really want to get a handle not only on the country but also downtown Boston. Randy said Officer Ryan was not home. I think either he or the commander got him back to work."

Stress really makes me tired. Dusk want setting in. Lighting candles would serve no purpose. We still had flashlights to go to the bathroom. Randy was outside. He set up warning string too. He had learned how in an old war movie. One would tie together two tin can with nuts and bolts in them. They would be spaced about ten feet apart. The string should not be seen. This way if someone was to go after the Buick we could hear the rattling of the cans.

Emotionally I was still distraught—too much for me to handle. I could get relief through a whiskey bottle, but a look at the drunk ended that thought. I was a father and a husband but also the glue for our collaborative. It was not only a means for our survival but also a good social interaction for all of us. When the patriot players came out for introductions, they came out as a team. They did not come out one at a time. They were one. This was what I wanted for the collaborative.

"Alice, I really need to get to bed," I stated boldly. "Tomorrow is a pivotal day."

"Sounds like good advice, Ben," Alice said with more normality.

In the middle of the night, I got up to go to the bathroom. Alice was sleeping on her back. She was not on her side with her back to me. *Huh?* I thought. *I do believe the war is over.*

I had a decent night's sleep. As morning came, the temperature cooled in the house. We were now at the same temperature as outside. Sleeping under a lot of quilts, your body stays warm, but your face breathes in the cool air. It does put me in a deep sleep. When I arise, I feel rested.

In the morning I found Randy awake. We both made some instant coffee. With the refrigerator cooled down, I opened it. I decided to scramble some eggs for the whole family. So far with our collaborative, we were staying afloat. I did feel a little sad. I knew we had taken action, and we were surviving; however, I was sure many of the elderly and those who lived in high-rise complexes were probably not so fortunate. I told Randy that I would be outside checking the sundial for the correct time. As the days passed in April, we found the sunrise early at 7:30 a.m. We had a meeting today set for the early afternoon. I wanted to cut as many branches as I could. I sat on my cooler for a half hour. I was enjoying my cup of coffee. The air was crisp, and the sun was magnificent.

I did hear the sounds of a cargo plane. The military must have been flying in supplies. The military and politicians made sure they were protected from all unforeseen events. We've known about EMP devices for a long time. It is a tradition that goes back a long time. *Save the queen and king at all costs.* There are underground bunkers for the top leaders. I wondered if our top leaders had evolved at all.

In my humble opinion, there have been three great leaders in this past century. First has to be Winston Churchill. The Nazi war machine rained down on London daily. As the stoic population sought shelter with each siren, Winston gave his famous speech. "There is nothing to fear but fear itself." It gave hope not only to the English but to all the Allies as well. They were hardened fighters.

My second pick would be President John Kennedy (Camelot). He was an Ivy League man who spoke eloquently. He was a Democrat and our first Catholic. His Boston accent made him distinguishable. He traveled to the Berlin Wall. In German, he told the Berliners, "We stand with you." He gave courage to those who defied the Russian communist machine.

What impressed me was his communication to the common folks. He urged shelters against a possible nuke attack. This was more symbolic than a real solution. The main thrust was to let those KGB thugs know we were ready to defy them. He implored all Americans with one of his most famous lines, "Ask not what your country can do for you but what you can do for your country." Gads, that was inspirational. High school and other public buildings display this saying in their foyers to this day.

Like the license plate of New Hampshire says, "Live Free or Die," he drew his line in the sand. During the Cuban Missile Crisis, he sent US Navy warships to form a blockade. President Kennedy was not about to let Russians install nukes ninety miles from Key West. As the Russian premier pounded his mighty fist, he sent the Russian submarines into action. They were there to possibly sink the American ships. It was an extremely tense time for the two superpowers. The most perilous time was when the Russian submarines lost contact with the

Kremlin. The world outcome was in the hands of a resolute American president and the commander of a Russian submarine. The Russian commander could have sent a torpedo at the Americans. That could have had started a nuclear war that would have devastated our planet. Only the cockroaches would survive the nuclear blast. The Russian commander was sane. He knew there could be no winners. He ordered the submarines to stand down.

President Kennedy had a love for his country and our forefathers. His policies were made for economic growth. On that frightful day in November, he was taken from us. The horror and emotions went into infamy.

The third great leader in my view was President Ronald Reagan—a cowboy actor, a former Democrat, governor, and finally president. When he became president, the country was in turmoil. With high inflation, Americans were taken hostage. We were humiliated and appeared weak.

The economy spiraled downward. The Russian bear was getting fat. It snarled and breathed down heavily on Europe. The Europeans seemed passive and splintered. The great communicator talked directly to the American people. He explained in detail about the threat to freedom, to us, and to the world. He came up with a plan—Star Wars, which was a giant money pit. It was a ruse, a bluff at the poker table. To the Russians, it was real. They tried to match him. But their economy was in a fragile state. The Russian people suffered greatly. The Russians then spent the final ruble that broke their economy. They could not empty their pockets of any more change. Like the walls of Jericho, the Berlin wall came down. There were rumors that the guards were confused with their orders. Some historians say it was a communication glitch. After the wall came down, there was a domino effect. The Eastern Bloc was fractured and floating away.

Like Kennedy, President Reagan had love for his country. He enacted his supply-side economic policies. With the far-left liberals and most of the mainstream media mocking him, he carried out his policy. He said with pure eloquence, "Rising seas lift all ships." This was his theme. The economic seas really rose in the United States. Trillions in wealth was created. There were so many jobs that people from around the world were trying to jump aboard our economic gravy train. He did this not for personal gain but love of all mankind.

After President Reagan, the American experiment hit many snags. We were adrift. The political monster reared its ugly head. Instead of speaking from the hearts, government filled with professional handlers. The right and left dug in their heels. The Beltway caught a terrible disease called polarization. Instead of a love for country, it was a love of money and power.

In my opinion we drifted without a rudder. Our top leaders became wealthy while they were in office.

Their families and friends became wealthy. All the while I viewed Moses on top of the mountain, shaking his head. He saw all this greed and domination for personal gain.

Here we are in a terrible predicament. There could have been a biological weapon, suicide bombings, and number of other threats. In an open and free society, it is difficult to protect the people. No longer wishing to reminisce, I had to deal with our collaborative. The hardships were very real. I wanted another fire—fire for warmth, light, cooking, and purifying our water. A fire with stimulating social discourse outweighs being alone in front of a TV tube. As a good Christian, I knew there had to be a light at the end of this tunnel.

It was late morning. Already the Henderson family and a few neighbors came. I just hoped the drunk would show up sober. To my surprise, Vivian and her mom showed up. They both came on bicycles. Vivian's mom indicated to me that she had to cook the meat in her freezer. It would go bad soon. I said to her, "Isn't it dangerous for two women to be out in this wasteland?"

"I believe Jesus will protect me, but I also have this equalizer," she said. Then she showed me a 9mm gun. I smiled.

We would soon start another collaborative meeting with good food. One could only pull the rabbit out of the hat so many times. I was sure with the survival radio would be spitting out a gloomy forecast. But today for us it was sunny skies.

It started out more as a frat party than a meeting. But a constant drumbeat of gloom and doom came out of the survival radio—countless stories of deaths, riots, suicides, and mankind's inhumanity to man. Just west of the Mississippi River, survival tents were set up. They were intended to stop the flow of immigration into the unaffected area. The whole country had been affected economically and spiritually.

Commerce, stock markets, and communications had been influenced throughout the whole country.

To make matters worse, biker gangs from Southern California went into the affected areas. They attacked the supply trucks to the tent cities. Just like Genghis Khan, they also went for the spoils. In this new lawless territory, there was one matter they did not count on. They were entering an area of guns and Bibles. To many of these simple people, they all had one common thread. There was no gray area. Either you were children of God, or you were doing the bidding of the Devil. After a while our new president did seem like a leader. When a convoy of supplies was sent, it was well protected. There would be no stagecoach sent out for the slaughter.

Everyone was here except Officer Ryan. We all chimed in and had a say. Even the drunk showed up and spoke with a coherent tongue. My God, would miracles never cease? We pooled our resources and ideas. I told everyone my plans for the following day. Right then Officer Ryan's wife showed up. She explained that he was called to duty. *Damn*, I thought, *there goes our mafia protection*. I told her I was about to embark on a short trip to a Boston hospital. She told me that if I could wait one more day, her husband would join me. It seemed that the barracks commander had a sick mom at a Boston hospital. When he found out about the Buick, he asked for a favor. Well, her husband smiled and said he would oblige. I thought about it for a few minutes. I told her that I would pick him up early the day after tomorrow.

"Please tell him to be dresses in his state trooper's attire. I do not want the Buick confiscated by another policeman or gang." She agreed.

We all agreed on this change in plans, and the meeting petered out as the day turned into night. It was another day to be thankful for. Again the drunk and William helped to keep the area tidy. Well, it was off to bed for me. I was also off to a more receptive wife. I insisted that Vivian and her mom sleep here for the night. I told them, "You got to know when to hold them and when to fold them." They both smiled and nodded. As Jimmy Durante would say, "Good night, Mrs. Calabash, wherever you are."

CHAPTER 4

Boston or Bust

THERE WAS ONE more day before my trip to Boston. Most times it is less than an hour's drive to Boston. When I would go to work in the morning, it could take me one and half to two hours. It is a small and compact city. The thousands of college students, hospitals, and churches really promotes gridlock in the mix. Many of the high-tech companies like mine are in the outer section of the city. With the Atlantic Ocean acting as a buffer to the east, all traffic comes from the other parts.

There are a few roads, such as the Mass Pike, that are straight. Many of the other roads wind and turn. This is a challenge to the snowplows. Many of the roads date back hundreds of years. They follow cow or horse paths. I do not know if the cows and horses were in search of water or if they had a drinking problem. Like so many cities, Boston has too many vehicles to traverse the limited roads. I thought there was a divine reason to delay one more day.

Officer Ryan seemed like a straight shooter, but was he battle-tested? I knew whatever talent he had was better than anyone in our little collaborative. Like a finely tuned engine, we functioned as one.

Eventually we would run out of some necessities, but I felt we were faring better than most. The trip through Providence and to Connecticut was a harrowing one. In my gut I knew there could be worse challenges in Boston.

My head was swimming with multiple thoughts. Right now my family and neighbors had food, water, and basic survival resources. It was the unknown that frightened me. I had accomplished keeping my wife and son fed and protected. It was security that I needed to provide them. We've walked on eggshells. I had a real thirst to listen to more to the survival radio. The more knowledge I gained, the better for me to handle our own survival. Randy and Alice could easily break out of the fold again. I had to really laugh at myself. Jessica and Vivian were more battle-tested than Randy or probably Officer Ryan. During my trip to Boston, someone will have to ride shotgun.

The good, the bad, and the ugly seemed to come out of all of us during this crisis. Jessica was solidly behind me. I hoped that there would be a fairy-tale ending to this ongoing nightmare. Every father dreams of walking down the aisle with his only little princess. I had to wipe away a tear in my eyes. *Why, Lord, do we have to have so much evil in the world?* It was not only the terrorist but men who beat their wives and dogs. It was the corrupt politician, all the Internet scams, and all the salesmen selling snake oil. The list went on and on.

As I was from Nebraska, I liked to keep it simple. As I got older, I tried to get a little wiser. The greatest line I ever heard came from President Reagan. "Trust but verify," he said. *Damn, that says it all.* Everyone's mind wanders when we are put to the test. I was a Christian man. I had learned much. The Lord would not throw anything at you that you could not handle. Thinking about pleasant memories relaxes people. William was always mediating. He was so mellow. Funny he didn't smoke pot, drink, or watch any kind of porn. I really respected him for finding that inner peace. To me, if there ever was a modern-day Moses, it would be him.

If a bad storm was headed our way, I could see him parting the Red Sea for us. He would keep it simple. He would say, "Follow me," and give no other words. The power of a few simple words is better than a filibuster on the floor of Congress.

Men—we are such simple animals. Keep our belly filled and give us the touch of a female. Bingo, that's the formula. I have tried to be a good husband at all times. Of course I looked at other females. Even President Carter has said he has had lust in his heart. He did not act on it, and neither have I. I really did miss Alice touching me. In time I was sure she would again. It had to be on her terms for it to feel natural. Now I was thankful to be alive. I was still dealing with that life I took. All the talk and condolences did not help.

It was only time. William had told me many times that our souls never die. Maybe in the heat of the moment, she chose the dark side. Before I slept, I touched my own Bible.

"Lord," I said, "I really need you now more than ever. Please, Lord. Please, Jesus, give me strength. This so very hard. I am really finding it difficult. Thank you, Jesus." I cried softly. I had to be strong for my family and neighbors.

I needed a good night's sleep. I had only one bathroom run. I always got up early. Living on a farm would do that to you. I ate oatmeal. Having eggs every morning was a bit much for me.

The collaborative was doing well. All of us had a good amount of veggies and bread, and for a few days, we had cooked meat thanks mostly to Vivian's mom. To go forward, I needed to listen to the survival radio and also get to downtown Boston. We needed a road map, a light at the end of the tunnel.

Alice was in the kitchen. She was talking to Jessica and preparing breakfast for Randy. I took the radio outside. The sundial showed 8:15 a.m. Human nature was a funny thing, In Nebraska, my neighbors came to me directly, and I would go to them. They would ask me directly, "Can we listen to your radio?" Here in the politically correct Boston area, there was a cat-and-mouse ritual—a casual passing, a casual nod, a slight glance from the distance. *Crap*, I thought, *this is a collaborative. I am not the despot ruler of the clan.*

It was time to end the dog and pony show, foolish games. I invited everyone who wanted to come over. It was a cloudy day in the sixties. "Mr. Henderson, you are one talented contractor," I said to him with deep respect. "With no power tools, you and your sons built a class-act well. The Buick and sundial have made this the apex of our temple. I know it is on our land. We have to respect one another. But, we need one another: Mr. Henderson and his tools, the efforts of all in a common garden even the food and good spirits of our next door neighbor.

At this point the drunk came by. God, I was beginning to like him. I was seeing an intelligent and sensitive side to him. Behind that thespian mask, there was a quality human. He felt like he was part of something. There was now a real hunger from all of us for information. Across most of America, there was a breakdown. Without communication, we were becoming lawlessness. Was there a power vacuum? Who was the new superpower? Would we be attacked again? Where was central control? I did not blame my neighbors. I was also curious. All of us listened. The president did give a short speech. He did announce that they now knew who committed this horrible event. He also indicated that ships from different parts of the West Coast and some NATO countries were on their way. When the ships arrived, they would prioritize.

MICHAEL KRAVITZ

"Prioritize? What kind of crap is that?" a neighbor screamed out. "My wife and kids played by the rules. We need to be taken care of. We need to eat and survive like the rest. Damn!" He ranted while he kicked up dirt.

As a union worker and loyal liberal, he really believed in big government and the big tent. He always had bumper stickers and signs on his lawn. He always joined the political rallies that the union pushed. I have never argued with him. No one could. Where your bread was buttered was how you voted. He really was a decent man. I just thought sometimes his Kool-Aid was spiked. No government could prepare for this disaster. Yes, the New York Stock Exchange was closed. The Chicago Mercantile Exchange was also closed.

After the president spoke, the rest of the news was mixed. Russia was feeling its oats. They pushed farther. The Chinese sent a few warships to Taiwan. Our new president was gutsy. He could have sent a few ships from the Seventh Fleet to help with relief efforts. If he did, it would signal weakness. Yes, the need to save American lives was important. There was a bigger need though. If we survived this attack, there would need to be a civilized world where we could live.

The Japanese and many other countries were on high alert. There was urgent and direct talk with our consul in Taiwan. The Japanese flew a high dignitary to meet with the top commander of the US Seventh Fleet. They meet aboard an aircraft carrier. When they signed the surrender agreement after World War II, the Americans sent only tall officers. It was a face-saving gesture to Japan. It signal that the American were more physically able. This supposedly gave comfort to Japan. In reality, a bullet doesn't care about your height. Our new president was showing signs of leadership. He sent a message to the commander. The Seventh Fleet was to stay put. In return, he pressured the government of Japan to produce survival radios and other electronic devices very quickly. Lives were at stake, and we needed to send a message to China.

Many of the NATO countries and other alliances put their air force and military on high alert. In the end it wasn't to come to America's aid but rather to protect themselves. In a power vacuum, the beast could smell the blood of a wounded animal. Russia's economy was still very weak. The Russians flying over US territory was a decoy. It was all a chess game. You could give up a few rooks to capture the king. Any territory Russia took over could be a further drain on their economy.

China was in a paradox. They were more pragmatic than what most would think. They were an economic powerhouse. With more than a billion people, they needed buyers for their products. News coming to them and the rest of the world was sketchy. Everyone knew that the mortality count was in the thousands. If it started to climb to the millions, it would be a game changer. Time was of the essence. Survival was a natural instinct in animals and humans. With high-rises, the elderly, and a politically divided nation, it becomes a complicated mess.

I was in as much need of information as the others in the collaborative were. We had a good thing going. All of us needed to know the big picture. Was our little well-oiled group surviving while a tsunami was ready to engulf us? It would likely take time to learn. Like newborn cubs, we needed to wander from our protective mom to seek answers.

"Damn, Boston is just a short drive," I said. "A one-hour drive on a Sunday morning. Now to all of us, it seems there is an ocean in our way. There still has to be a government entity at the big gold dome. I promised Alice I would go to the hospital to check on her mom. Jessica knows the war zone around our little parameter. Alice and Randy have yet to be exposed to these realities. I have informed our little group of my venture tomorrow. I will pick up Officer Ryan at 8:00 a.m." Randy wanted to come, but I told him no. We could only afford to let one of us to go at a time. The family and collaborative had to survive at all costs. Randy understood.

When one becomes emotionally drained, it is physically draining. With darkness now approaching, the sundial was of no use. It was still too early to go to bed. "Screw it," I said. I made a couple of sandwiches. One was peanut butter. I made the other with the meat from Vivian's mom. I knew I was not supposed to sleep right after eating, but I was emotionally done for the night. Tomorrow morning I would just drink instant coffee and eat toast. Practically speaking, I did not know what bathroom outlets would be available to me on this trip. With my wife and children, no problem, but Officer Ryan, I am not sure.

I have enough on my mind already. I didn't need to worry about my bodily functions. It was off to bed. Actually I enjoyed sleeping with a little cool, crisp air. I was half asleep when Alice crawled into bed. She said, "Good night, dear. Please be careful. The collaborative needs you." She paused. "I need you," she said with a slight tremble.

In my sleep I heard her words. It was comforting, and I really needed to hear it. She still didn't touch me, but we were making progress. My face showed a slight smile as I dozed off.

It was a good night. I had sound sleep with just one trip to the bathroom. First light I was wide awake. The toilet still worked, but the water pressure was slowing. If we did lose water pressure, we would resort to the bucket brigade. Everyone would have fill buckets with water every day to fill the back of the toilets. At least there was a well for everyone in the collaborative. I wondered how the high-rises are faring. I got myself some instant coffee. This morning I took just two pieces of toast. My mental state and my constitution were in good shape. The sundial said it was almost 7:00 a.m. I put a little more gas in the Buick. Randy had done a good job keeping the gas cans filled. Both the Buick and generator were kept in a good supply of fuel. The Buick was still in a showroom display. He would always use high-grade oil. In the new cars, many used the synthetic oil. The Buick was all polished.

Everything seemed like a go. I walked back to the house. I thought I would arrive a little early at Officer Ryan's home. Fifteen feet from the front door, Alice came out. This was a little out of character. I stopped in my tracks.

"Hi, hon," I said with a little cheer.

"After you went to bed, Jessica and I talked," she exclaimed in a solemn tone. "I have always been closer to her than Randy. I love them both. It's just sometimes females communicate more in an emotional manner than men. I know she finally bonded with you."

"This has been a really tough time for me," she continued in an apologizing tone. "I always use Jessica as a sounding board. She does the same to me."

"What are you getting at, Alice?" I said with a confused and anxious manner. "I have to go meet officer Ryan for our little trip," I said with a little impatience.

At this point she walked up to me. She put her arms around me and started to cry.

I was in total shock. I didn't know how to react. She cried for several minutes. I put my hands on the back of her head.

"Jessica saw something in you that I always knew," she said and then collected herself.. "That you are strong, sensitive, caring, and good under adversity. She is now a daddy's girl. Even Vivian and her mom can see it." She wiped away a tear. "I know it was dangerous. I know this trip to Boston could be worse. I need you to know how proud I am of you and how much Jessica, Randy, and I love you. Please be careful."

Her touching me was utopia. I was now vulnerable. I had to be in a good state of mind for my trip. I wish I had an hour or two just to be alone with her. Reality was a bitch. I knew the trip had to move forward as scheduled. *What should I say?* I needed to instill confidence that everything was going to be fine. *What if I don't come back? Should I make peace with Alice and the kids?* Maybe I should have written a letter in case I did not come back alive. I collected myself. The Almighty had a path for me. If I had had these doubts a few hours ago, I would have written a letter. I put my trust in him. I knew he would keep me from evil.

"Alice, you been a great wife and mother," I said with a loving tone. "God has blessed me with two great children. Somehow Officer Ryan is my guardian angel. Either he or someone through him is going to be my protector. I don't know why I feel this way, but I do. It is not often I get these strong feelings, but when I do, they are always right."

Alice nodded in approval, her arms still around me. "I know you are right," she exclaimed. With her right hand, she grasped the back of my head and gave me a long and loving kiss. Next she pressed herself hard against. It was as if we were one. After a good twenty seconds, she grasped my two arms and kissed me on the cheek. "You be careful, Ben. You be very careful," she said with a strong and commanding voice.

At this point I had to turn around quickly. I did not want her to see my tears. I had to show strength. Maybe it was a man thing. There were a lot of things I could have said to her, but my mind turned quickly. I had to show confidence and a little leadership.

As I walked a good ten feet away, I collected myself. "We have a lot of stops. I will not only go to the hospital, but I have to make a few stops on officer Ryan's behalf. I should be home by dusk. Love you, honey," I said proudly without breaking down.

I was on my mission. I got in my car and started the engine. *Damn, it purrs like a well-padded kitten. Randy really has a masterpiece with this Buick. Just one broken side mirror.* Officer Ryan house was just two miles away. It was three maybe four minutes away by car, and I arrived a good fifteen minutes early. It was a small but well-kept ranch, and I pulled in his driveway when I got there. The grass and hedges were growing.

Unless he had a simple lawn mower, he would have to let the lawn go just like the rest of us. I turned the key off. Officer Ryan came out. To my shock, another police officer came out. He was tall and a good ten years the senior to Officer Ryan. Not only was he in good shape, but his uniform was clean and pressed too. He had a short haircut, and he was clean-shaven. *Damn*, I thought as my stomach got a queasy feeling.

Bones called Spock in his little communicator. "Spock here," he said.

"Beam me up, Spock," Bones said with clarity.

"What is it?" Spock answered as he sat in the commander chair aboard the *Enterprise*.

"There seems to be a few humans in unbelievably pristine attire in this nuclear disaster of a planet," Bones said in an unmistakable tone.

"Hmm, not logical," Spock said. "You need to find out an explanation before I will allow you to beam up. Spock over and out," Spock said with authority.

Damn, what the f---. Both Ryan and his friend had two duffel bags.

"Good morning, Mr. Randal" Officer Ryan commented with a strong and confident voice. "This is Lieutenant Mallard. He will be joining us today." It was as if I had no say in the manner.

"Good morning. Nice to meet you," the lieutenant said with a voice of a strong leader.

The lieutenant signaled to Officer Ryan. "Oh yeah, I almost forgot. I'll be right back," Office Ryan said in an obliging manner.

Officer Ryan went into his house and came back with two large banners.

On a light blue background and printed in dark blue, the banners read, "State Police." Each one also had the state seal. Both Officer Ryan and Lieutenant Mallard attached each banner to the front and back of the car. *Damn*, I thought. *They are commandeering my car. Just two miles from my house, I am being bushwhacked. I need to call the posse (my collaborative) for help.* If I had had a whistle and they could hear it, they could come to my rescue. They would make it a few hundred yards. Most were out of shape and would collapse before they made it to William's house. Most of them would be moaning and breathing heavily by then. They would simply say, "Forget about it. Ben is on his own."

"Mr. Randal, Officer Ryan has told me a lot about you," the lieutenant said.

I had a lump in my throat. *Here we go.* It felt like I was flunking a test or being dumped by a pretty girlfriend. *They're going to take Randy's car. I'm outgunned. Besides their guns are bigger than mine.*

"We have a symbiotic relationship. You need to get into Boston safely, and I need a ride for official business. I need to get to government center, and you need to get to a hospital in Boston," he continued with a direct and informative tone. "Were you in the armed services, Mr. Randal?" he asked..

"Yes, I was. US Army … three years. And you, Lieutenant?"

"I was in special services … and trained as a sniper. Two tours in Iraq," the lieutenant said with a slow and modest tone.

Both Officer Ryan and the lieutenant had side arms. Officer Ryan took a shotgun with him. The lieutenant had a rifle with a scope. The bullet would follow his red line.

The lieutenant sat in the front passenger seat and Office Ryan sat in the back. I had bookends—two Captain Americas. Will Smith just had one when he tried to take the exam to become an agent for *Men in Black*. I turned over the key. Randy sure kept this fine machine tuned.

I pulled out of Officer Ryan's driveway and onto a side street. There were not many cars on this end of the street. "Mr. Randal, please take a right here," he said as if he has a Sears, Roebuck & Company license.

"You know every time when we secured land in a hostile area, we made sure there was a main supply route. That route was always well guarded," he said in order to keep me informed. "Napoleon, Stalin, even here in the blizzard of '78, we did it. That route is a lifeline. Right now I know the best way to get to downtown Boston." There were also some very bad people who knew this information.

At this point I was more receptive to the lieutenant giving me directions. He tried making small talk. He asked how long I had lived in Boston and if I missed Nebraska. At this point his pressed uniform and haircut were gnawing at me. A little four-inch angel appeared on my left ear. She was dressed in a white rob and halo over her head. "You need to be informed," said the four-inch angel.

Next a four-inch devil appeared on my right ear. He was dressed in black and held a fiery fork. "You can't afford to be informed," hissed the little devil.

The white robe angel with the halo put her hands on her hips. She had a stern look. Next she drifted up a good six inches. She was over my head and in direct line with the devil. She took out a ray gun that was almost half her height. She vaporized the devil and then drifted down to my left ear.

"Spock says, 'Not logical.' You need to be informed," whispered the little angel.

Damn, you're right. I need to be informed. How do I do this? Should I do it in the politically correct way? I have to do a little song and dance. Maybe I can ask the lieutenant if he is going to the finals of the mud-wrestling tournament. Or maybe I can offer him front-row seats to a Gallagher show. Gallagher likes to smash watermelons with a sledgehammer. I looked at his big gun. *Screw it. I am from Nebraska. I'll be blunt.*

"Lieutenant, if I can be so bold," I said slowly and firmly

"Yes, Mr. Randal," he commented with complete confidence in himself.

"How is it when we are in a nuclear containment zone? Everything electronic and electrical has ceased. Millions of cockroaches are spiking the footballs. It's halftime, and you come out of the locker room. You have a new pressed uniform, a haircut, and a shower shave. It's like you're on a different channel than the rest of us." I finished my tirade with trepidation.

With a slight chuckle, the lieutenant answered, "You see, Mr. Randal, when the nuke went off, I was in shock and as stymied as you were. I checked with my neighbors. Cars, radios—there was nothing. The next day my commander bicycled down to my house. You see, he is an exercise fanatic."

Under my breadth, I said, "Like the lieutenant is not obsessive about his physique."

"The commander had a secured Faraday line. It was a FEMA protocol. He explained what happened. He told me that this was no drill. There were priorities that were in place," the lieutenant explained clearly.

"Well, Lieutenant, thank you," I politely answered as he pointed for me to take a turn. "Sounds like your commander at the barracks is reading the same cue card as the president," I continued as I dodged another stalled car.

The lieutenant laughed as I went between a few more stalled cars. "Pharmacies, hospitals, nursing homes, the elderly—I guess the list is pretty large, wouldn't you say, Mr. Randal?" The lieutenant talked like he was the adversary. "You see, Mr. Randal," he continued as he pointed to another turn. "It is the correctional institutions that this commander was most concerned with. Many of the guards did not show up. We also had many troopers that did not show up for days. Those who did not report after three to four days were considered AWOL," he said with great authority. "To serve and protect—that has to mean something. If not, then we are doomed as a proud and free country."

"Officer Ryan and I went to the correction facility," he said with a little anger in his voice. "It was extremely tense. Some of the inmates became extremely violent. For several hours our lives were on the line. The warden and I had to make hard decisions. We both agreed that 35 percent of the prisoners had to be set free." He pointed for me to make another right. "The warden was brilliant. The prisoners that were set free were offered a choice. If they stayed and helped, the warden would offer them a clean CORI if our country would get back on the grid." "Oh, as for my duds and haircut," he then said. "We have several gas generators. Snow and ice storms always knocked out the power. Morale has to be kept up. The laundry room and kitchen still functioned a few hours a day. We have to care for them, or the riots will really intensify. Food and water are rationed. The state has a limited supply. A few ships will arrive shortly under the cover of darkness." He pointed for me to make yet another turn.

Boston was just like many other cities. They had an outer beltway and inner beltway. Driving on the outer beltway would allow us to bypass most of the heavy traffic. However, it was a longer route. Once you crossed into the inner beltway, you were coming to outskirts of the city. This was standard with most cities on the East Coast. We were crossing that inner beltway now.

"Mr. Randal, please turn down this residential street," the lieutenant commanded

As we turned, several brick apartment buildings came into view. As we came up to the one on the left, the three of us saw something very sickening. In the parking lot of the apartment building, there were stalled cars. Perhaps up to three-fourths were still empty. Many had left that morning for work or school. Toward the end of the parking lot, we saw three corpses.

All the apartment buildings in Massachusetts were under rigorous regulations. Very seldom would one see debris lying around. The Board of Health gave out warnings and then citations. There were also a lot of fire and building regulations. This really created a large expense to the landlords. In turn, they had to figure this cost into the rents. There were constant evictions and many hardships. With a low-paying job, one could not afford these high rents.

Now there was litter everywhere. There were broken windows and a dreadful stench. We drove very slowly. We could see the corpses and a scrawny dog.

All the corpses belonged to young male. One was white, and the other two were minorities. The sickening part was there was a dog grabbing the arm of one of the deceased. The dog was trying to pull the body, but to no avail. It was scrawny and desperate. Lieutenant Mallard told me to pull in. Within fifty feet of the dog, he ordered me to stop. He slowly exited the car.

Never taking his eye off the dog, he walked slowly toward it. The scrawny dog sensed the intruder. Slowly the dog turned its head. Then crouched and snarling, the dog dug in. It seemed that this was his.

At this point he pulled out his revolver. To me, all life was precious, even that of animals. A rabid dog, a sick dog, or a dog that draws blood is usually put down. Some animal lovers would take their animals across the state line to New Hampshire. It seemed their laws were different, which is strange because New Hampshire was a lot more conservative. They just seemed more lenient with dogs. In Nebraska, I always lived with dogs. They served not only as pets but as a warning system too. When I moved here, I never wanted a dog. The homes were too close. The highways were busy, and neighbors complained about barking.

As you enter New Hampshire, it is all congested. In a short drive, the houses spread out. It is a different existence than Massachusetts. The snowfall and cold are much more extreme. It really is a state for the outdoorsman (or woman). There's snowmobiling, hunting, hiking, camping, and shooting. It is a beautiful state, but when the fall leaves turn color. It is really God's panoramic shot. Parts of New England and Japan have the best color changes in the world.

I did not cover my ears. I could not look as the lieutenant put the dog down. It was just one humane shot. He then walked to the car and signaled to Officer Ryan. They opened the trunk. The lieutenant took out two body bags. He also had gloves and two masks. The two officers put their masks and gloves on. Office Ryan had a small bag of a white powdery substance. With great respect, they placed two of the three in body bags. Officer Ryan sprinkled the white powder on all three bodies. My guess was that it was lye. It would kill the scent so stray animals wouldn't go after them. Both Officer Ryan and the lieutenant placed the bodies at the end of the parking lot.

The lieutenant picked up the casing to the spent cartridge. He slowly walked back, wearing a very solemn look.

"Mr. Randal, your best guess as to what time it is." He took out his pen and notepad.

"My best guess it is 9: 30 a.m.," I told him with confidence.

The lieutenant wrote down the time. He walked out to the street to see what landmarks he could see. He carefully drew a diagram of the building and where we would leave the corpses. *Man, this really sucks. I just wanted to check on my mother-in-law and give a ride to the two officers. There is no rubbish being picked up, no traffic.* To me, this was not normal. We were in a highly populated area. There should have been countless people walking around.

The noise of the spent bullet did seem to draw attention. As we looked up at the various apartments, we could see people looking out from the windows. The lieutenant was very savvy. He told us that he would walk from here. He went back into the trunk and pulled out two bulletproof vests. He put one on, and so did Officer Ryan. I looked at the lieutenant with a little anger.

"What am I? A sacrifice? An expendable, useless chauffeur?" I said as I looked him in the eye.

"You worry too much, Mr. Randal." He went into the trunk and pulled a third bulletproof vest. "Really, Mr. Randal, you will be the safest of the three of us," he said assuredly.

"Why is that?" I asked as I put on my chest protector.

"There are some very bad people who know we are here." He got his rifle with the scope on it. "They want your car more than they want weed, crack, or anything else. Your car is the granddaddy. It is one thing that they can use to make themselves feel really important," The lieutenant said as he checked his rifle and his sidearm.

"Should I get the shotgun out?" Officer Ryan asked the lieutenant.

"Yes, I will start walking first on the left side of the road. You will be behind me on the other side. Stay around fifty behind me," the lieutenant said. It sounded like he had done this before.

"Mr. Randal, you stay fifteen feet behind Officer Ryan. You should be fine. They want the Buick without bullet holes. That means they have to go through me and Officer Ryan. They know if we are going into Boston, we are also coming back this way," he said without much emotion. "I have dealt with a lot worse."

The lieutenant started to walk, looking through his scope. When he got about fifty ahead, he signaled for Officer Ryan to start walking. I was very tense. The lieutenant was at high alert. He seemed very confident. After he walked a good twenty minutes, we saw a few of the young gang members. They were on top of the roof of a four-story brick building.

First there were three. The lieutenant signaled for us to stop. Then five more came out. Damn, there were eight of them all with 9mm guns. No wonder there were no people around. This was a lot worse than Providence. They were all young males, mostly minorities, but two were white.

"You'd better be bringing that Buick for us. These are our streets," their leader said.

The lieutenant, who was as cool as cucumber, raised his rifle and walked toward them. *God, what big brass ones he has.* He stopped about sixty feet in front of them.

"Go ahead. There aren't enough of you. I am fast and extremely accurate. He turned on the red beam. Instead of shining it against the leader's head, he pointed it at the man's chest. This way he could see the beam on him. Four of his followers turned tail and ran. "Come on. Let's get this over with. Your gang is going to need a new leader in five seconds." The lieutenant took complete control.

He started to count loudly and fast. Five. Four. Three. At this point they all left except for one. He was a big dude, not the leader but definitely a bully and thug. The lieutenant pulled out his revolver and ran after him. As he entered the door of the building, Officer Ryan ran to the front of the building. I pulled the Buick closer. I held on to my rifle. After a tense three to four minutes, the lieutenant came back out.

"All clear. They are cowards. They like to terrorize innocent people. They figured we were a special tactical unit," he said as he continued to look around. "I have been ordered not to shoot unless they shoot at me. That is a bunch of crap. This is the main road coming in and out of Boston. We are in a state of emergency. These maggots have to be dealt with. The commander and governor needs to know how grave this is."

We traveled another hour on foot. There were no people for almost a half an hour. Finally as we got closer to downtown, we started to see people walking on foot. Up ahead we saw a barrier. Behind the barrier there were several personnel members from an army guard unit. The sergeant signaled for us to stop.

"You made it through the little war zone," the sergeant said as he walked around the car. "Open up the trunk please." He checked the lieutenant and Officer Ryan's IDs. "Nice Buick," he said as he was finishing his inspection.

"Somebody has to help those civilians that are trapped back there," the lieutenant said to the sergeant." If something is not done soon, they will die. They are afraid to come out of their apartments for fear of being robbed and shot."

"We know the situation is bad. We have orders not to shoot at civilians unless someone shots at us. There is also a jurisdiction problem. Someone has to explain this to the governor. We are trying to get a few armored units that work," the sergeant remarked as he waved us on.

Driving from this point on was safe. Hundreds of people were walking and milling around. Traffic consisted mostly of bicycles and Rollerblades. We saw a few vintage cars too.

Like ours, most have a state police banner on them. Hopefully they had not been confiscated. I really was afraid to ask. It might open up a box of worms. We drove at a slow pace.

It was weird. Hundreds and hundreds of people eyed us. Both the lieutenant and Officer Ryan pulled their revolvers out. They both kept them in their laps. All of us were nervous about any kind of flash mob. I had never seen so many young coeds. I think Randy could have had a field day out here with his Buick. I knew I had to keep this to myself. He was a good boy. I didn't want him to turn to the wild side.

The whole area seems to be clean. There were many volunteers wearing armbands. They had various duties. Some were cleaning the trash. Others were trying to move the stalled vehicles out of the way. At least the inner city seemed safe. When we drove within a mile of the government center, we saw two lines of people. At the end of each line, there were local police with rifles and dogs. It was a food line. It was a basic meal of meat veggies and very little meat. Good water seemed to be in short supply. I would be afraid to give the city water even to an animal. The other line was a heck of a bit shorter. It was a VIP line for volunteers with armbands.

I did bring two bottles of spring water. Man, I did not realize how valuable that water run turned out to be. I was using one for the three of us, and I would use the other to barter with when I reach the hospital. The day was cloudy with light rain. Here in Boston, there was a somber dress code. At least it was today. Light jackets and sweaters seemed to be the rule. The state color should have been gray, not blue. College kids and yuppies dressed a little cheerier. Most big money people, like lawyers, doctors and financial analysts wore gray or black suits. It was the musicians and professional athlete who dress to kill. Their outfits were like big neon signs that said, "Look at me. Aren't I great?" The doctors, lawyers, and financial wizards tried to stay under the radar. After all, they took a good part of our money.

After a few more miles, we are at the government center. It was another emotionally draining trip. Survival was taking its toll on all of us. No small talk, just silence. No radios, just the car engine. It was almost like being among the walking dead. After several more minutes, we came to another barrier. This time it was the inner sanctum of the deal makers—the nerve center of our state. It was like being in the green zone of Baghdad. We had to park our car and proceed on foot for the last three or four blocks.

The street was blocked off. The staff removed out the stall cars. The area was made into official parking lot with twenty-four-hour security. There was only one way in and one way out. Guards with rifles stood at both exits. There were several other vintage cars and vintage motorcycles. There were also two cruisers from Bangor, Maine. The EMP must not have affected them. Everyone who parked here needed an escort to the governor's office.

"Mr. Randal, Officer Ryan and I are going up to meet with the governor," the lieutenant said to me as he received a receipt for the Buick. "The hospital that you want to go to is about a twenty-minute bike ride from here."

"Bike ride? What the hell!" I said in bewilderment.

"Yes, Mr. Randal, a bike ride. You are gracious with your car. If you drive and park your car there, it will be gone within a few minutes. I will send a patrolman with two bikes. One for you and one for him," the lieutenant said with a firm voice.

"But I have a gallon of spring water and a little food to barter with the doctors," I said.

"That's fine. We have baskets for carrying parcels. It is a common thing," the lieutenant said as he started walking away. "We'll meet here at fourteen hundred hours."

"You mean 2:00 p.m., Lieutenant? We're not in the military anymore," I said, but I doubted he heard me. *How the crap do I know when two o'clock is without a watch or cell phone?* I thought. *This is really getting complicated.* Why couldn't we keep this simple? I could drop the two officers off and go to the hospital. I would check things out and get back to Alice by lunch. Now I had to wait for a patrolman and take a bike ride. It felt like I was part of the Brady bunch. Right now I could take a shot of whiskey just to calm my nerves.

I waited for close to thirty minutes in a parking lot with guards that look like they could be serving at Buckingham Palace. At least they could have let me back onto the main street. There was no TV so that I can look at the coeds. That could have made for thirty minutes of blissful memories. God created those pretty little creatures so that men could smile. Once they smiled, the dentist could say, "Oh boy, do you have a credit card on you?"

I looked up, and there was the patrolman with two bikes. Mine had a basket in the front. At least it was not a woman's bike. In this politically correct world, anything would fly. Even Milton Burrill, a famous actor, dressed as a woman almost a century ago. It was his shtick. I did not care for it, but it was accepted then. Nowadays it's like Sadie Hawkins day occurs multiple times a year.

The patrolman handed me the bike with a basket attached. We also had two chains with locks on them.

"You have a .22 rifle with you," the patrolman said as he pulled out a strap. "I don't think you will need it around here, but it is good to have. If anyone did see us, they would likely back off." He also gave me a light jacket with state police on it. He indicated to me that it would make this venture less complicated, which was music to my ears. He was in good shape. He was middle-aged but not a jock. It looked like he ate donuts with his coffee. At least his morning coffee. God gave me a reprieve. No more Captain Americas. If we ever get back to normal, I would have two quests. One would be to find that Indian chief from Connecticut and thank him all over again. The second would be to find each of the policemen who helped me and buy them a cup of coffee. In honesty, the lieutenant had gained my respect. I wished they still had the red light district. I could buy him two tickets as a thank-you gift. Knowing him, he would arrest me for corruption.

Multitudes of people all stared as we biked past. Food and water were on most of their minds. The patrol man peddled only to meet my speed. He could undoubtedly beat me in a short- or long-distance ride. As we rode, I noticed that even a few miles from the green zone (my interpretation) was clean of debris and cars. Food and water were the driving forces … along with boredom.

As we came up to the hospital, I could see the guards in front. There was also a desk outside with a chair and umbrella. The triage nurse was sitting outside. We both dismounted our bikes and walked to the front. The patrolman told me to be quiet. He would do the talking.

"Hi, we are here on official business," the patrolman said.

"Fine," the triage nurse said. "No guns inside. Only correctional officers with prisoners. They must have a seal from the warden. We are in a state of emergency" she declared. "I am very sorry. We are understaffed. The doctors and nurses who did come back are anxious."

The patrolman could absolutely identify with her. The governor's office was also understaffed and overworked.

"Mr. Randal, I will wait here with the two bikes and your rifle," the patrolman said. "You have forty-five minutes. That's it, and then we've got to bike back," he said as he looked at a watch someone had loaned to him. It was giving, along with two patrol cars, from the Bangor Police Department.

"Got it," I said as I got the water and food that Alice had prepared for bartering. I entered the hospital. *Damn*, I thought, *what a smell. It seems more like the Bates Motel than a hospital. First thing's first.* I had to urinate badly. I found a bathroom that worked. I had not used a bathroom since 8:00 a.m. No Dunkin' Donuts or Starbucks.

The police were with me at all times, so I could not go behind a building. The bathroom smell was bad. But Mother Nature held the trump card. I stepped up to the urinal and kept singing, "Oh, what a relief it is."

Then I washed my hands. Damn, no paper towel and no hand blower. I washed my hands anyway. The hospital still had hand sanitizer. That constant noise from gas generators would drive anyone nuts. The few nurses and doctors were all running and looked haggard. I asked several nurses and one doctor to find Alice's mother. No one knew. No computers or phones made the situation very challenging. I was finally directed to the third floor. The intake staff could possibly help me.

"Can you help me locate a patient please?" I politely asked the staff member.

"I am not sure. Give me a name, and I will try," the staff member said.

I gave her Alice's mother's name.

"She is eighty-three, five-foot-three with a slight figure," I described for the man.

"I remember her. She was due for a bypass surgery. The doctor was having a hard time with the limited staff and equipment. We have not seen the doctor for the past two days," the staff member said with a bit of sadness. "I can direct you to a resident doctor. He was learning and practicing under him," the staff member said, trying to help.

Carrying my gallon of spring water and food, I located the resident doctor on the second floor.

"Excuse me, Doc," I said firmly. "I am the son-in-law of an eighty-three-year-old patient you had." Then I pulled out my ID.

"Yes, I remember," he said with his head down." She was to have a simple bypass surgery. We could not line up enough support technicians and equipment to do the operation," he said softly. "The doctor was called into another hospital that had everything in place. I am very sorry. She passed away without pain. We spend our lives trying to save people. Now we are forced to make hard and painful decisions. She is down in the basement. We are running out of room for the deceased," he said with a tinge of anger. "We can smell the corpse up to the third floor. We have gas generators. We need someone to handle the deceased."

"Doc, I need syringes and insulin. It is for a seventies-plus diabetic." I held my hand over my face with disbelief.

"We have a protocol to help the younger people first. It is from the surgeon general in Washington. I think it is from the past administration," he said calmly.

"Look, Doc. Fresh spring water and also some freshly cooked food. I will trade it for thee syringes and insulin." I still had my hand on my face. "Really, Doc, water and food represent life. Syringes and insulin will save a life," I said in a determined way.

"All right, Mr. Randal, you have gone through a lot," the doc said with compassion. "Here is a slip. The pharmacy is on the second floor. Do not mention the age of you friend." As he accepted the water and food, he said, "I do not make the rules. It's not my pay grade."

God, the pain did not end. There was a battery clock on the second floor. I had ten minutes left. Alice was in a fragile state. This was going to be hard on her—not being with her mom when she passed. I ran to the second floor. The pharmacist said he would be with me in a few minutes. He was filling a few other orders.

"Look, there is a police escort outside from the governor's office. They want me out there in less than ten minutes. They are very strict. Go look for yourself," I said to the pharmacist.

"Here, Mr. Randal." He came from back of the room." These syringes will work. We do not have the insulin the doctor wrote up. I am giving you a different one. It will work, just not as well as the other one. One is for an older person," he said as if to get rid of me.

I started to panic. I only had a few minutes left. I ran up to the front desk.

"What happens to the deceased?" I said

"We store them in the bottom floor. A technician is trying to preserve them, My guess is they will be put in a pauper's grave. It is not a good scene. There is a careful log of everything," the receptionist declared.

I ran outside. The patrolman was still there.

"You're two minutes late," the patrolman said as he looked at his watch. "How did it go?"

"Mixed, very mixed," I answered him as I put the package in my basket.

I slung the rifle over my shoulder and mounted my bike. We were off. Both of us peddled a little fast. The 2:00 p.m. deadline was coming fast. It was all right weather for a bike ride—cool with on-and-off rain showers. We biked by hundreds of people. There were no incidents.

We pulled into the parking lot. The lieutenant and Officer Ryan were both there.

"Good timing, Mr. Randall," the lieutenant said as he walked over to the Buick.

I took the package out of the basket. I handed back the bike to the patrolman. I wanted to kiss the Buick, but I was sure they would think I was weird.

"Mr. Randall, one more stop before we go back," the lieutenant said.

Both had bought their duffle bags back. I think there was a good exchange.

The lieutenant bought some plans with him. He also came back with a few need supplies.

As I entered the Buick, I put the package under my seat. I put the rifle on the dashboard.

I could get at it right away. It was also a signal to any potential thugs. The lieutenant directed me to our next stop. It was another hospital. This time we were visiting his commander.

It was a good ten-minute ride from where we were.

We saw the volunteers with the armbands. They were trying to move some more stalled cars out of the way. It was hard business, but these streets were a lot easier to navigate. We came up to the front entrance of the hospital. Mostly people were walking, but with the state police banners, we just parked out front. They had a similar setup. The number of people trying to enter the hospital had greatly increased. With guards and a triage nurse outside, they could weed out a lot of people. There was also a staffing problem. Many nurses, maintenance men, janitors, and even a few doctors did not show up. Without proper equipment, salaries, and public transportation, there was little incentive to show up.

The lieutenant said he needed thirty-five to forty minutes inside the hospital. Officer Ryan and I waited by the car. As the lieutenant headed inside, I noticed a large gathering about three to four blocks away. I told Officer Ryan I would like to check it out. I would stay in eyesight of him. I grabbed my keys and took my rifle with me. I slung the rifle over my right shoulder. I was not going to leave the keys with anyone, period. My family, collaborative, and my self-worth depended on those keys. Before we used to never leave home without a cell phone and your AAA card. Now it came to even a simpler need—a rifle and a set of keys. It was sad. It was one small step for the one who set off the nuke … and one giant step backward for mankind.

I walked toward the large group of people. There was a large screen on the side of the building. Damn, some tech nerd hooked up a small generator. As information came in over the survival radio or by some other secured means the nerd's video setup made it public. Information kept us sane.

It prevents anxiety and connects us to the outside world. Man, how hard was it for Lewis and Clark? They set out to explore without any contact. I was very careful. I did not want to be jumped. I did still have the state police jacket. Next to me there was a tall African man. He had a slight build and short haircut.

I said hello to him, and he spoke in broken English.

"I am from Kenya, and I came to win my big check," commented the polite Kenyan.

"Big check?" I asked with curiosity in my voice.

"Yes, a very big check. The winner of the Boston Marathon receives a very large check," he said with a slight sadness. "I have trained very hard. I was in the hotel when the nuke went off."

"What happens to you now" I asked with compassion.

"Our consulate is at the same hotel as I am. We have contacted the Canadian embassy. They are sending three buses down from Montreal. As a courtesy to Boston Marathon, they will donate two of the buses. I will leave with several other foreigners."

"That will be good for you," I said with upmost admiration.

"Yes, it will be great. Electricity, TV, transportation, food, newspapers, I miss it. America, so many people dream of coming here. I hope you can bring back your greatness," he said.

I said good-bye to him. It had been a good fifteen to twenty minutes. I hoped when the lieutenant came out, he looked at the hospital clock. The staff there had the ones with batteries in them. I opened the front door. I took off my rifle and put it next to me. I kept the keys in my left pocket. I did not want to hurt Officer Ryan's feelings. It wasn't that I didn't trust him. The keys were just extremely sacred. Only I and Randy were to touch them and have them—period.

The lieutenant came out with a smile on his face.

"Good news," Officer Ryan said with a jubilant look.

"Yes, very good news. She is doing well," said the lieutenant.

I had mixed emotions as I started the Buick. Alice's mom was gone, and I had to tell her. Still I was haunted by the death of the angry bitch. And we still had to traverse the war zone to get back.

We traveled for several miles, and now we were at the outer barrier. We stopped the car for the guardsmen. They had to inspect all of the vehicles coming and going. They wished us good luck and Godspeed. The lieutenant did inform them that he had a talk with the governor's top people. They had several vintage cars, motorcycles, and a few army vehicles that had Faraday protection. They would soon bring in rice, water, bread, and a squadron of highly trained force. The governor knew that this main route needed to be protected.

As we drove off, the lieutenant said to Officer Ryan and me, "I told the governor that if he gave me the green light, I could handle this in one night. I think he was afraid of his poll numbers. We started to drive slower. There were less and less people. It became very quiet. I drove even slower. Occasionally we saw an window open. All the people felt terrorized. I wanted to tell them that help was coming tomorrow. If we did that, these thugs would start breaking into their apartments tonight.

We passed the area where we saw them last. The lieutenant signaled us to stop. This time he played it differently. He walked on the left, and Officer Ryan walked on the right. I followed close by, driving very slowly. Ten minutes went by, and there was nothing. We were still on high alert. We crawled around the bend. Then those dark evildoers came out of the shadows. The lieutenant sprang into action. If we were too defensive, they would pick us off. The lieutenant ran toward them. He stopped and put his finger in his mouth. The he checked the wind direction. This time he saw the same big bully. Instinct told him that he was the head of the snake. We knew that if we cut off the head, the snake would die. It was a real dilemma. There were hundreds of people inside those apartments. They would become future witnesses of whatever happened.

The lieutenant knew this. He had to get the bully to shoot first. He was a good one hundred feet away. It would be an almost impossible shot for the bully with his 9mm. The lieutenant knew it was a shot he had made hundreds of time. He waved his hand toward his face. He was egging the bully on to take a shot. Even an Olympic shooter would have a hard time making the shot. Nothing happened. The lieutenant stepped in another ten yards. He held the rifle with his right hand. He waved his left hand toward his face. This time Officer Ryan got a pair of big ones. He walked up to the lieutenant and then pointed his shotgun at the bully.

In reality, a shotgun at this distance was useless, but the rifle with the red light was a game changer. Officer Ryan stepped another five feet to the side. The bully was now in a cross fire. The other maggots were backing off. The lieutenant really wanted to pick him off. However, if he shot first, the truth would come out later. It would have been the end of his career. There were no face-saving measures for the bully. He was mad. He lowered his gun and waved his hand in a disgusted manner. This bully was pure evil, and the lieutenant needed to let the proper authorities know.

His two tours in Iraq had taught him a lot about the streets. Evil was evil. You couldn't talk to evil or reason with evil. If you didn't eradicate evil, it would spread. Officer Ryan and the lieutenant walked back to the car. This time the lieutenant sat on the hood on the passenger side. Officer Ryan sat inside with the window open. I drove at fifteen miles per hour. It was a lot faster than walking. At this speed the lieutenant could handle the lookout. After several hundred yards, the lieutenant signaled for me to stop. He got inside. Now I could drive at normal speed.

Honestly I didn't want to go through that again. I have always respected our soldiers who fought to keep us free. They deserve the best we can give them. We approached the first inner beltway. We were now safe and headed home. I was not sure of the exact time, but it must have been a little after 4:00 p.m. It was an eventful day. I was really sad about Alice's mother. If the tactical team showed up tomorrow, it would be great. The lieutenant had a Faraday line in the barracks. He had a good friend who would be on the patrol too. If a convicted killer escaped from a prison, there were different rules of engagement. The authorities could shoot first.

All three of us felt this bully had already taken innocent lives. All of us thought that the three corpses were the result of the bully's actions. I felt the governor would give his friend the go-ahead. Even though I was emotionally drained, I had accomplished a lot. Many lives would be saved. I wanted to go back to Alice and my family. No more house calls just mail in the money the doctor said.

CHAPTER 5

Homeward Bound

WE HAD JUST crossed over the inner beltway, and we were leaving Boston. The three of us gave sighs of relief. You could see the relief on the lieutenant's face. He was more relaxed, less stressed. His expression was even better than it was on the day I gave him some of the spring water.

One can last many days without food, but not without water. In the city there were hundreds of people who are afraid of coming out of their apartments. The city water was still running, and I hoped they were using gas generators.

I was happy with our collaborative. We just had to feed and provide water to about a dozen families. Taking care of thousands of apartment dwellers would be a nightmare. There was no way they could feel as free as the three of us did right now. But I had to tone down my concern for them in order to survive. All I could do was help and pray for my family, our collaborative, and those who would become part of my path in life.

As we were driving, I could hear the engine of a military cargo plane. There was a base not far from our home. The military tried to get a variance to expand many years ago. The neighbors fought them hard. In the end the air base gave up. How sad. Now we could definitely use it. It was odd not seeing those small puddle jumpers flying. Almost everyone lost contact with the control towers when the nuke went off. Some of the experienced pilots landed in fields and highways. Many had unhappy endings.

The mood in our car was relieved but still solemn. At this point I no longer needed directions from the lieutenant. We just took our turn off the main road. As I weaved in out of stalled cars, I noticed Attorney Schiller's house. He was out there with a small push lawn mower. He had all the time in the day to do his own maintenance now. After a few more blocks, we arrived at Officer Ryan's house. As I pulled into his driveway, his wife heard the car engine and came out to greet us. I turned off the engine and grabbed the steering wheel with both hands. It was like I had to hold on to something before I allowed myself to let out a sigh of relief. Officer Ryan and the lieutenant thanked me. I was anxious to see Alice and the kids. I said good-bye and started up the Buick for the drive home.

As I backed out of the driveway, I hesitated to look both ways for other cars, even though I knew that there were no other cars around for miles. Old habits were hard to break. As I proceeded in the direction of home, I first drove to William's house. Fred was outside. He was still cursing the squirrel. I stopped my car, and William came out to greet me. I handed him the package of syringes and insulin. He was quite excited that I could secure them. I kept the engine going.

"William, I am sorry I cannot stay. I have some unpleasant news for Alice," I said. "Stop by tomorrow at noon. We can talk and listen to the survival radio." Then I drove off.

William just nodded, and I proceeded on down the road to my house.

Home sweet home. Alice, Jessica, and Randy came out to see me. Randy checked out the car very carefully. He put his hand on the Buick. It was like his woman. He cared for it very lovingly. "Ben, glad you came back. All of us were nervous," Alice said with a sigh of relief. "Were you able to get everything accomplished?"

"Yes, Alice, everything." I held my head low.

"Mom? What about Mom?" Alice asked, her hand over mouth.

"I am very sorry, Alice. This is as hard for me as it is for you." Then I looked her in the eyes.

"Why? How? I don't get it. She was in for a routine bypass." She was in shock and denial.

"I know, Alice. I know. I thought the same way," I said slowly. At this point Alice broke down. She really cried for many minutes. I just let her go on. She needed to find some closure. "I did talk to one of the doctors. They couldn't get a team together. They also did not have all the equipment that was needed for the operation. There were a high percentage of operations that were canceled," I said, choosing my words carefully.

"What happens now with her, Ben?" she said as she wiped tears from her face.

"I asked that question at the front desk. The clerk said that all the people who have passed will be carefully logged. They are going to put everyone in pauper's graves. They can only keep all the corpses for a short time," I said, and she started to cry again.

"My mom deserves better. She was a good woman, a loving mother."

"You're right, Alice. It is not only her. It is many people," I explained, trying to make sense of this mess. At this point I walked up to Alice and hugged her. Jessica and Randy, both sensitive to the situation, hugged their mom for several minutes.

Randy took the keys from me and moved the Buick to the back. I knew he was ready to check the oil and the tires. Even with the trip to Connecticut and Boston, it wasn't enough miles to do an oil change. He knew I was responsible with his car, so I went directly into the house. Alice had supper on the table for me. I told her I really needed something strong to calm my nerves. She brought out a shot of bourbon and set it by the lit candles on the table.

Tonight I would just let her be with her emotions. After I talked to Jessica and Randy, it was time for bed. Somehow all the words in the world wouldn't make a difference. It was only time that could heal these wounds. I did tell her that when it was safe, we could have our own little service at the grave. I held her as we slept.

I was up early. Alice still slept. She had been crying most of the night. Finally when she was exhausted, she fell asleep. I was as quiet as I could be. Temperature was not too bad. It was probably in the fifties.

The gas generator ran a good forty to fifty minutes a day. Alice and Jessica were able to do ironing and use the microwave. As quiet as I could be, I went into our wooden dresser drawer. I pulled out clean clothes. After yesterday's episode I needed a shower. Damn, shaving and showering in cold water really sucked. It was a fast shower.

Breakfast consisted of pasta between two slices of wheat bread. At least Alice had mixed in some veggies. I put an overcoat on just to get the chill out of my body. A cold shower and dressing in a chilly home didn't cut it. I heated up an instant coffee. Usually I was the first one up. Jessica was also an early riser. I was in fairly good shape, maybe just twelve to fifteen pounds over my ideal weight. This past two weeks, however, my calorie intake was way down.

I walked outside. The air was crisp, and the sky was blue. In the burbs there was little pollution. Now there was hardly any traffic. The air should be even cleaner, except for some radiation. On the survival radio, I didn't heard any mention of the air though.

Off in the distance, I saw one of our collaborative members. She was a divorcée of average height, and she watched her food intake. She was easy on the eyes. Her daughter was also very attractive. Randy had seen her too, but for some reason, they hadn't spoken to each other yet. Her ex-husband loved his daughter, but he was a womanizer. It reached a point where the mother just couldn't take the humiliation anymore.

Randy definitely liked females, but he was a little awkward around them. The divorcée's daughter suffered emotional damage from her father's behavior. He never mistreated her. He just didn't show up when he said he would. She seemed traumatized by this pattern. But she liked men, even though she didn't trust them.

I waved to the divorcée to come join me. I had a milk crate and water cooler to sit on. She was dressed for gardening. We talked about growing a larger vegetable garden. She indicated to me that if others could help her, there would be a lot of food for the collaborative. I smiled and said, "That's a great idea."

At this point Jessica was up. She had her coffee in hand. "Morning, Dad," she said with a beautiful smile. "Morning" she said to the divorced lady.

"Come. Join us, dear. Trust me. It's the only game in town," I said, trying to keep the mood light. She sat to my left, using me as a buffer. It was fine. At least I had showered. I wasn't wearing deodorant, but I was good. I loved my wife, but this was good therapy for me.

Jessica had really bonded with me. On her wedding day, I will undoubtedly break down. Now I needed to get Randy out of his shell. *Hmm*, I thought, *if we get back to normal, perhaps I will get him a round-trip ticket to Amsterdam. I'll tell him to do some window shopping. That should do it.*

"Jessica, we were talking about growing a large vegetable garden," I said to bring her into the loop. "If only we had a chicken farm. Then we would be self-sufficient," I said jokingly.

"Count me in. I would love to learn about growing a vegetable garden," she said to the divorced lady.

"Done then," I said as I slapped both knees. I think I'll gather more wood for a bonfire again."

"That was a great night," the divorced lady recollected. "I am delighted your wife went in the tub first. It is good to see you have a good marriage," she said in an approving manner.

"Dad, can we sing some Taylor Swift or hip-hop music this time?" Jessica said. "Neil Diamond? Really, Dad?"

I was going to say something, but she would understand later in life. *Wait till she starts paying bills*, I thought. I paused for a moment and commented, "Honey, you can show us your talents tonight. I will get the Hendersons to help with the well water again." At this point Jessica only showed a half smile. She thought the world of Mr. Henderson. She just wanted to keep away from his son.

I finished my coffee, and I excused myself. I wanted to make sure we had enough wood. I knew that others would show up after noon. As I started gathering wood, Alice came outside. She had a coffee but no food with her. We all handled stress differently. Some just gouged themselves, while others did not eat at all. I was not entirely sure what I could say to comfort her.

"Morning, hon" I said. I gave her my recognition but left the tone of conversation up to her. She looked at me.

"Morning," she halfheartedly said. She sat down and looked past me. "It doesn't seem fair or real to me," she said in a despondent manner. "There was never a mean bone in her body. There is so much evil in the world, and God takes away the good. The people who set off the nuke—I wonder where their souls are," she said with bit of anger.

I continued with my wood gathering. Somehow, trying to comfort Alice with words seemed counterproductive. She has to deal with the memories and the proverbial why. *Why did the nuke go off now? Why did my mother not go last year? Why couldn't we get a hospital outside of the city? Maybe I should have gone there right away. Maybe I could have demanded or taken her someplace else.* She would beat herself up for days and maybe weeks. The constant why would play out over and over.I needed to give her some space.

After my trip to Boston, I was thankful to be out in the burbs. Our group seemed proactive. There was not only camaraderie but a real feeling that we would pull through this. Each day we heard the engine of military cargo planes. There was activity. Many of the cities along the East Coast were a lot larger than Boston.

Mr. Henderson usually dropped by around noon. I raked out the pit and readied the wood. I made a temple out of it. Air had to circulate in and out of the wood pile. There was a good perimeter around it. This way there would be no forest fires.

The sundial showed that it was a little past 12:30 p.m. when Mr. Henderson showed up with a six-pack of beer.

"Must be past noon, Mr. Randal," he commented, trying to determine if I would have a beer with him.

"It certainly is," I said as I started to salivate. "Why not get a bucket of cold water from the well, and we can put them in there. But just put four of them in. I can use one now." Alice went back into the house. In another hour people would come with the generator.

We both sat down and engaged in a few minutes of small talk. I raised some necessary points. "If we are going to survive, this collaborative group we need common goals. There has to be a list. All of us should have a say." After a few minutes, my next-door neighbor, the drunk, showed up.

"Afternoon, gents," the drunk greeted us both.

"Afternoon," both Mr. Henderson and I said in return.

"This is a first. Starting the party without me?" He bought out his bottle of whiskey. He looked at his watch and looked at the sundial. "Damn, this sundial is pretty accurate."

"Have a seat. We are going to have a little meeting if enough show up," I commented. At this point Jessica, Randy, and William came over and sat down. "After the meeting I will start the fire. We can cook and heat up some water for washing and bathing." I said to our little group.

"I'd like to clear out my can goods. I can't even walk in the room," the drunk said in a helpful manner.

"Let's go. Randy and I will help bring out some of the cans. Why don't you put down the bottle of whiskey? You can drink it later," Jessica said. She had taken on a new admiration for the drunk. Hopefully she could instill a new purpose for him in his life. Randy grabbed a wheelbarrow. They went off to the drunk's house. Jessica had really had an effect on him. I hoped it would last.

It was hard for the rest to tell time. I decided to start the fire. I really wanted to get the meeting out of the way. I put my beer down. William helped light the fire. After a few minutes, the fire was roaring. You could see the flames for several blocks. Instead of using a cell phone, I could now send up smoke signals. Wow, I actually learned something watching those old westerns. It worked. Everyone showed up except Officer Ryan. He was likely called to duty.

As we started the meeting, we heard another cargo plane. The military seemed serious about bringing in supplies. Mr. Henderson's son told us about an army truck going to the center of town. The routine had been going on for two weeks. Many people were surely without food. The town water was still running. The taste was bad though, and I was not sure it has been tested.

"This is our meeting, everyone. We need a list of goods for our survival. Anyone want to start?" I said, trying to get things started.

"Does anyone have a pair of hair clippers? We can cut hair once a week. While we run the iron and refrigerator, why not cut hair?" Alice said as she decided to be proactive. She looked at me and smiled. The death of her mother was taxing on her. She knew I was trying to keep everything together. She did not want to add more weight to my shoulders. Besides, it was good for her to get a break from her heavy grief once in a while.

It wasn't long before several members offered some great ideas. This was the first time I could take a break from leading the collaborative. Now it was working on its own. After several minutes of good ideas, it turned into a good old group therapy. No one knew about the inner problems of others. It seemed everyone wanted to clean their own souls. Even the liberal union worker confessed his little bubble had busted. For the first time he saw that the politicians usually took care for themselves first. They were still living large while we suffered.

Many of our emotions came out. We were all suffering together. No longer were we competing for better jobs and lifestyles or trying to show that my house is better than someone else's.

It all reminded me of an old sitcom that my father liked. I didn't watch the realty shows like Alice and Jessica used to. My father loved the *Bob Newhart Show*. Our therapy session reminded me of one particular episode.

His landlord, Mr. Carlson, walked into his office. His hair was scuffled. He had a sport jacket on, which was not much of a fashion statement. He leaned against the receptionist's counter. He was talking to her but not looking at her. He always saw the glass as half empty. He seemed well off financially, but he was always bored. He liked to meddle in the affairs of the others. The receptionist was tall and statuesque. She often sat at her desk and filed her nails. She liked one-liners that had a little sarcasm. These were two people talking to each other but not listening.

Bob Newhart walked into the office. He was going to have a group therapy session. That moment seemed like what we were doing now. He asked Mr. Carlson if he would like to join in. Mr. Carlson, who was bored, always wanted to know what Bob Newhart did, so he agreed. Bob Newhart shut the door. The receptionist continued with her nails. Mr. Carlson sat somewhat in the middle of the group. Bob sat opposite everyone but faced them. He started the session off. Everyone started to pour out their hearts and problems. Instead of joining in, Mr. Carlson looked at everyone. He was amused. He did have a remark to everyone. In today's politically correct society, his blunt and somewhat tasteless comments would not be accepted. Everyone looked at him and then continued with the session.

After the meeting was over, he asked Bob what he charged for a session. As he looked at Bob Newhart, he said, "That's a lot of money just to talk." He indicated that he would have to increase Bob's rent. I always carried the recollection of this episode my whole life. We can always misjudge others by just looking at their external appearance. It is important to look into their souls. This is the place where the true value of any human resides.

Our little collaborative had grown emotionally tolerant of others. It was great. The fire was going strong. All of us were well feed. Many took baths and washed their clothes. We did have the survival radio for those who had a yearning for the latest news. Our health and spirits were strong. Deep down we all knew that something was going to happen.

California's economy is larger than the economies of most countries. Combine that with some of the closest states, and you still have a viable country. The government would not allow the relocation of millions of people. With Katrina, the government contained them in a large superdome. I found that sad. The government was still pouring over all of the options. The lack of news is what caused such high anxiety.

This night passed without any drama. The drunk had a timepiece that worked. I really wanted to get to bed. A lot of stress made me tired. Mr. Henderson made sure the fire was under control. He kept a buffer around the pit.

After I had been around the fire for several hours, my whole body had warmed up. Then I climbed under the covers. It felt great. Alice came in after a few hours. I thank her for the support before I was off to my dream world.

I did sleep well. There were no noises from cars. Looking out the window, there was just darkness—no streetlights or house lights. A few of the neighbors did have candles or battery lights. Because we were getting closer to May, I feared the hot, humid weather. In the Sunbelt, the situation would surely be dire.

Most mornings turned out to be the same. We would have coffee with a little milk or powdered cream. Today, however, William came by. He and his wife had several creams. He gave me one. He appreciated the insulin and syringes. He did inquire about the army truck that a few people had seen. I told him, "I believe it is only a matter of time before we received help. The logistics of helping millions must be a nightmare." William agreed. He did not want to leave Fred unattended for a long time, so he decided to go back home. It was hard to gauge the weather. The skies were ominous. Late April could bring many rainy days.

It was hard to read the sundial when it was cloudy out. My best guess was that it was a little after nine in the morning. Jessica was up and trying to clean around the living room. Randy was not up yet. He had a good time talking to Mr. Henderson's sons. I personally thought he should have at least acknowledged the divorcée's daughter. *The next time I see the divorcée*, I now thought, *I will suggest that her daughter and Randy start on the garden. Damn, am I good.*

I didn't know if it was going to rain. Alice would be up soon, and I decided to start another little fire. When Alice got up, she could make some soup. I liked to read some of my textbooks too. An outside fire would keep me and others warm. It was so much better being out in the burbs than it had been navigating downtown Boston. I started the fire and went in to get a book and a few manuscripts. It was not a day on the beach, but to me, it was close. A half an hour into my self-indulgence, I heard a strange sound like that of a two-cycle engine. The noise was getting louder and closer.

I got up from my water cooler. (It was the best seat in the house.) As the noise got louder, my curiosity overcame me, and I jogged to the road. In the far distance, I could make out two objects coming this way. Truly this was an event. Two antique motor bikes with two people on them kept coming in this direction. They came right toward me. Soon their engines and speed were slowing down. I was stunned! It was Officer Ryan and the lieutenant. They both stopped and smiled. They extended their kickstands and shut off the engines, and then they approached me.

"Collaborative, Mr. Randal, you are the talk at the barracks," the lieutenant said with a big smile. "You got the fire going well. Very impressive. I came here to introduce to you a few distant neighbors."

The lieutenant was trying to use me as a model collaborative. At this point Mr. Henderson came by. He had also heard the noise of the engines. I offered them some water from our well, but I instructed them to boil it first. It would be a long walk with a wheelbarrow to cart the water back if they could not get a vehicle. The Buick was around the back and out of sight. Both the lieutenant and Officer Ryan said nothing of the Buick. They could have commandeered it, but both had too much honor to pull a stunt like that.

The skies were starting to open a little, and the drizzle came. The lieutenant offered to pick up Mr. Henderson the next day. He could show them how to dig a well. With drizzle increasing, they were in a rush to get back. The lieutenant and Officer Ryan took off with their passengers.

After I went back into the house, the intensity of the drizzle increased. April showers may bring May flowers, but it was not much fun when it was damp and cool outside and a little cool inside. Alice was up, and we exchanged hellos.

We had a fireplace, but our careers had a way of limiting our time, so we never used it. I checked the flue, hoping that the liner inside the chimney was fine. Without electricity, our furnace did not work. Randy and I went outside to fetch some kindling. The rain was now coming down a bit harder. Back inside we took off our shoes so that we did not bring in dirt. Alice really liked a clean house. Wet wood made starting a fire a little more challenging. Finding old newspapers and other papers we no longer needed, we were ready to start. At first we smoked out the house. Try, try again. We crumbled up some newspapers and put small pieces of wood in the fireplace. Then we finally had our cozy fire going.

For the rest of the day, we traversed in and out of the house and looked for wood. This was a lot of work. I had to use an old saw to cut many of the pieces. This was a lot of work, but we had all the time we needed. Today they did not bring the generator. The rain not only dampened our feelings but limited our activities. Without opening up the refrigerator much, we survived the day. The girls did the cleaning. Randy and I read by the fireplace. Without lights, we headed off to bed early each night.

The next day was warm. Normally Randy would be watching the Sox play. Tickets could be costly. Randy told me that they could run in the hundreds. Parking, eating a Fenway frank, and drinking a beer could almost equal a mortgage payment. We had gone to a few minor league games. Parking was easier, and there seemed to be better interaction with other fans. At the end of the games, many times there were fireworks. You could get a good value for your money.

What a grand day. Our neighbors had survived. I saw a few up and about. I took a short walk and saw the divorcée. She was busy starting her garden by hand. Using a pick and hoe, she turned over the soil. With coffee in hand, I said hello. I mentioned that Randy and her daughter might be willing to help. *Interesting*, she thought. She wanted to dwell on it for a few days. She also said a few of the others would like to help. After a bit I headed home. Alice came out of the house with coffee.

The temperature both inside and outside of the house was pleasant. After a short time, we saw two figures coming down the road. It wasn't long before we could see it was Vivian and her mom on bicycles. Vivian seemed fine, but her mom looked like she should have taken a cab. She was really breathing hard because she was out of shape.

"Morning, Mr. and Mrs. Randal," Vivian exclaimed.

"Morning," both Alice and I politely returned.

"Morning, Vivian," Jessica said as she came out to greet them.

Randy came outside and said good morning too, but then he just sat and drank a cup of instant coffee.

"Mr. Randal, I came here to ask a favor," Vivian's mom said as she was holding onto the handle bars and breathing heavily. "I need a ride to check on my sister. She is alone. I think it would be better that she come stay with Vivian and me."

I hesitated and then sighed." I am not sure. I have been through two harrowing experiences. I don't think I can go through it again," I said with as much compassion as I could.

"She lives fifteen miles from here. It is not in Boston. I don't think I can bike that far," she said, still catching her breath

"I'm sorry. I think I reached my limits with taking drives outside our area," I said. I was still recovering from that last emotional trip.

"I can do it, Dad. It is safe where she lives. It's not the projects or downtown Boston," Randy said cheerfully.

"No, I do not think it is a good idea," I retorted, not wanting to put my son through what just happened to me.

"I understand, Mr. Randal. You have been through a lot. Maybe it's my turn. I have to try." Vivian's mom mounted the bike.

Vivian was about to speak herself, but her mom said that it was time for them to go.

"Stop. Please stop," Alice screamed out to Vivian and her mom as they were peddling away. Alice looked at Ben and then at Randy. "I just lost my mom. My heart is broken," she said. "I don't want to lose any of my family." As she carefully looked at all of us, she turned and looked at Vivian. "My dear, I would never forgive myself if you lost your mom on this bike ride." She walked toward Vivian and clasped her cheeks. "Randy, you be careful and come right back home. You know your dad and I will be worrying the whole time."

"I'll go with Randy. This is too much on my mom," Vivian interrupted.

"Besides, I have the equalizer. It will be the remake of *Butch Cassidy and the Sundance Kid*," Vivian said with a little naïveté.

"I—" I started, but Alice put her finger on my mouth.

"Randy will be fine. You're a great dad. You taught him well," Alice said.

"Yes, Dad, I will be fine," Randy said as he went to grab the .22 rifle. "Besides, I am really itchy to do something." Alice gave Randy a couple containers of food. I decided to give Randy two gallons of the spring water. It could be useful for bartering.

Jessica hugged Vivian, and Alice hugged Randy. Randy filled the tank with gas. All of us knew that Randy and I could not be together. When a calamity happened, the president and vice president always traveled separately. This way control and command could go forward. Randy had his .22 rifle, and Vivian had her gun. I had a knot in my stomach. Vivian's mom was in the backseat. They had to drop Vivian's mom off at her apartment complex. It was hard for me to watch. We were a Christian family. Alice and I had been through a lot. This was one more adventure in these troubled time.

Randy drove into the gated complex. Someone had crashed into the gate. The rubbish and the smell were a little bit much for his liking. Randy stopped the Buick by the side door. He lifted the bikes out of the trunk and let Vivian and her mom walk the bikes up to her apartment. To leave the Buick unguarded would be a tragic mistake. As he watched the two go upstairs, he noticed the rubbish that was strewn everywhere. There were several people looking at his car. Mostly they kept their distance. A few came up to engage him in conversation. Randy elected to keep a little distant. There was nothing to gain by being overly friendly with any of Vivian's neighbors. After a good ten minutes, Vivian came downstairs and out to the car.

"I am all set, Randy," she said as she opened the door. "Let's rock and roll." She closed the passenger door and put the gun in her lap.

"You'll have to give me directions," Randy said as he started up the Buick and drove past the broken gate. Vivian pointed for him to take a left. She was handling the gun.

"I hope I do not have to use it." She remembered the Providence incident.

"I hope not either," Randy said with compliance. Randy and Vivian had never interacted much. They were a few years apart in age, and she really was Vivian's friend.

"A lot of stalled cars and broken windows," Randy said.

"Yes, it was that way when we came back from Connecticut. It just seems that a few people are pushing the cars off to the side," she said when they noticed a few people trying to do just that. Vivian knew the way well. She took Randy through several side streets. "I am taking you around the side streets. I think there are a lot less stalled cars. The highways were packed early that morning, but not the side streets."

Doing it this way took longer. It was a good forty-minute ride. Randy noticed that they were in a section of town known as "the lower end." There were mostly three and six family wooden structures there. Some of the mom-and-pop stores were trashed. Some were sitting in chairs outside, guarding their stores.

"We are getting close," Vivian said as she noticed a few young kids milling around. More thugs looking for spoils. "It's a half of a mile past that pharmacy." Outside the pharmacy two police officers were standing guard. Randy noticed the young thugs. His instinct was to stop near the police officers. They were both middle-aged and African.

With one variety store trashed, the other had a man guarding it with a gun.

Randy rolled down the window. "Officer, we have to get to an apartment down the street. Could I get one of you to assist us?" he asked when he noticed that the number of thugs had increased to five. They were eying his beautiful Buick.

"What is a rich white boy doing in this part of town?" the African-American policeman said to Randy with an undertone of sarcasm.

"This is my sister's friend Vivian. Her aunt lives on the second floor three streets down," Randy explained, trying to work past the policeman's bias. "Look, I am just trying to get her aunt out of there and take her back with us. I will give you a gallon of spring water and some freshly made soup my mom made this morning. To top it off, I have an extra loaf of wheat bread." Randy was trying his best to bribe the tall policeman. Randy sighed, put his hand on the steering, and was about to take off.

"Just go with him," his fellow officer said. "Make sure your back in twenty minutes. We have our orders to guard this pharmacy. Just leave the water and food here," he said with wide eyes.

"Gladly," Randy said as he put the water and food on the sidewalk. The African-American policeman looked down at Randy's .22 and Vivian's gun.

He put on a bulletproof vest that was next to him on the ground. He picked up his shotgun and checked the safety, opened the door, and got into the backseat of the Buick.

"My mom died last week," he said while he was looking at the punks. "She was in a nursing home. After the blast went off, many of the workers did not show up the next day. The owners came back the next day with two wheelbarrows. They emptied the kitchen and never came back. Nobody cares about the poor anymore," he said with anger.

Randy just looked at him through the rearview mirror.

"At least you're trying to help," the police officer said, looking into the mirror.

"Pull over here and stop," Vivian ordered.

Randy stopped and turned off the engine.

"Let's go, Randy. Hurry up," Vivian said loudly.

Randy opened the door and grabbed his rifle. As he was getting out, he turned around and grabbed the keys. The police officer stepped outside the car. As he grabbed his shotgun, the punks started to come closer. They were drawn by the shiny Buick.

"You need to step back," the police officer shouted.

Two of them came closer. He took his shotgun and fired a round over their heads..

"I'm not playing," the officer exclaimed.

Randy was trying to get inside. The front door was locked. He knocked loudly. Nothing. Randy knocked even louder. Still nothing.

"Let's get going," the police officer yelled. "You've have ten minutes, and I am out of here."

"Screw it," Randy said. He lowered his shoulder and rammed into the door. The latch broke, and they were inside. Randy ran up the stairs as Vivian followed. He knocked on her aunt's door. Nothing. Vivian knocked twice very loudly. "Auntie? Auntie?" she said. There was a dark and narrow staircase. The walls were scuffed from furniture and appliances.

"Watch out, Vivian." Randy once again lowered his shoulder. It was an old wooden door. One hard run, and he was in.

"Auntie? Auntie?" Vivian yelled. Then she found her on the kitchen floor. "She is still breathing." Vivian gave her a small glass of juice she found on the counter. "We've got to go, Auntie. My mom will take care of you. We've got to go now," Vivian said with authority.

She turned. "Randy, get a few bags. Put some cans and dry goods in one. Take a few of her personal belongings and clothing too," she screamed.

"I can't find any bags," Randy exclaimed.

"Just grab two bedsheets," Vivian yelled even louder.

Randy grabbed two of the bedsheets from her bedroom. He saw some little critters. *Yuck*, he thought. He could also smell urine. Uncomfortable with woman's clothing, he threw in underwear and various blouses, pants, and skirts.

"Hurry up, folks. These little maggots creep me out," the police officer said.

Randy quickly put the other sheet on the kitchen floor and started the throw in canned goods and dry goods. He didn't even want to open the refrigerator door.

"You want to check what I threw in here?" Randy asked Vivian.

"No, Mom has a lot of clothes, and so do I," Vivian said politely. She grabbed her auntie by the shoulders and guided her downstairs.

Randy followed quickly. The police officer opened the door and helped with her aunt.

"My bankbook and health card are in my top dresser drawer," her auntie cried out. Randy just ran back upstairs. He opened the top draw and then took a pillowcase off the pillow. He put all the papers inside it. When they got to her sister's house, they could sort it out there.

"Let's go," yelled the police officer.

Everyone got into the car. Vivian's auntie was in the backseat with the police officer. Randy made a U-turn and went back to the pharmacy. The thugs were caught by surprise. They just stood there, especially since the police officer had his shotgun pointing out the window. Randy drove up to the pharmacy and pulled over. He just shook his hand. If he hugged him, he might have given him bedbugs. He just wanted to go home and shower. He would leave his clothes outside and wash them at the next collaborative meeting.

"Thank you, Randy," Vivian sincerely said. "You helped my mom and my auntie. You're a sweet guy. You're going to make some pretty girl happy one day."

With a big smile, Randy drove off to Vivian's mom's house. There were lots of stalled cars but no more calamities. They had been away for a little more than two hours. As Randy drove into the complex, he beeped his horn. Vivian's mom rushed out to see her sister. She started to cry, and she rocked her back and forth with a big hug. Vivian's mom had blue dungarees and a sweatshirt on. One of her friends was visiting. They each had a glass of wine. Vivian and her mom both hugged and thanked Randy.

"Tell Jessica I'll visit her in a few days," Vivian yelled out as Randy got in the Buick. With her auntie's belongings on the sidewalk, he started to back out.

"I will do that. Take care," Randy exclaimed. It was a very short drive home from there. Maybe ten minutes. Randy thought it was good just to take a drive.

As he passed the attorney's house, the air seemed crisper and cleaner. Or maybe his mind finally felt relaxed. When he went by William's house, he saw Fred outside, and the man waved to Randy. Randy beeped his horn, which made his day. Little human interaction really made Fred a happy man.

As Randy drove in, he beeped his horn once more. Mr. Henderson and the divorcée were in the yard. Everyone was happy to see Randy. He grabbed his .22 rifle as he exited the car.

"No gunshots, son?" I asked with curiosity.

"No, Dad, pretty routine. Just a warning shot from the police officer."

"Warning shot? Police officer?" I said. "What the hell did you two do?" I asked.

"I did what you said, Dad. I bartered with a police officer. He took the food and water. In return, he fired his shotgun in the air. It's like a male dog urinating on the bushes to mark his territory. That's all, Dad," Randy said as he took the rifle to his room.

With a big smile on my face, I thought, '*The apple doesn't fall far from the tree*'. It was time to start an outdoor fire so that we could all eat and warm up.

"Son, the divorcée is trying to till the land for a garden. When you're rested, why don't you help her? They sure could use a man helping once in a while," I said with utter politeness.

"I am on it, Dad," he replied.

As I turned around, I saw Alice hugging Jessica's shoulders. "God, I have two good men in my family," Alice said, wiping away a tear.

"Isn't that the truth?" Jessica said with a fond look on her face.

The rest of day went smoothly. Randy did take a cold shower. Because he was a little paranoid, he put his clothes in a plastic bag. He put them outside for someone to wash them. Randy knocked on the door of the divorcée. He helped her, and he interacted with her daughter. Both seemed a little guarded, but it went well. At least they were on the same page.

The weather started to get warmer. May can be a paradox in the Boston area. Trees were blooming, and green shoots were coming in everywhere. Officer Ryan drove up in his antique motorcycle. He thought the other collaborative was doing fine. They learned from our playbook. He stayed for several hours. We cooked a little and listened to the survival radio.

Officer Ryan did say some supplies were coming in. Thousands had lost their lives. The first shipments were slated for the sick and elderly. There was a tent city up and running in the middle of Maine. You needed a note from the police or your town office to go there. The staff would get you some supplies—laundry soap, rice, beans etc. If I wanted to share with others, he might send a policeman to accompany me. I told him that I needed a few weeks of calmness. I knew that with supplies dwindling, I would have to do something.

'Lie' a very sick patient, we have stopped the disease from spreading further.

"Listen, Officer Ryan. Let me be blunt," I said. "I know that your commander has a Faraday system in place. The town hall and the state and federal government all take care of themselves first," I said, choosing my words carefully.

"Our forefathers wanted the power to be with the people, not the politicians. There are more communication radios, phones, and other things being shipped either by our government and other governments. Why not let each little district elect their own people? They can set up the radios and communications themselves. This way we can control some of our own destiny," I said.

"You have been a true leader, Mr. Randal," Officer Ryan proclaimed. "I know the lieutenant and the governor's office have a lot of respect for you. All of us who are in the public sector don't always realize this. I myself forget it sometimes."

Officer Ryan continued, "Our pay and job security make us separate from most of you. All of us forget who is working for who. I will definitely pass on your sentiments. I do hope there is a light at the end of this tunnel."

"I hope so too, Officer Ryan," I retorted. "You know how Randy likes his football. If we ever normalize, wouldn't it be great to see a Patriots football game. At halftime the real event will be their mascots. They are dressed as patriots. They can march to the middle of the field and shoot their muskets."

"You have vision and eternal hope, Mr. Randal." Officer Ryan said as he mounted his antique motorbike.

"What do we have if we don't have hope?" I said to Officer Ryan.

Officer Ryan started the bike and gave me a salute as he drove away.

EPILOGUE

EVERY NATION HAS a tipping point. During the French Revolution the queen uttered her famous words: "let them eat cake". She lost her head; powerful words indeed. For our nation the powerful words say: "*It's the economy, stupid.*" The kettle had reached its boiling point.

Ben has risen to the occasion. They are surviving with a mixture of the present, and values one would find in the 1800s. Our government already has a big tent—social security, food stamps, Medicare, etc. They are starting to outnumber the workers. It's like a team of horses pulling a cart. The cart has much weight on it (our national debt). One horse is tired, so you put him (or her) on the cart, which means less horses pull the cart and there's more weight to pull. Add the heft of an EMP attack, and we can't survive without the help of more horses.

With his master's degree, Ben is anxious to work again. With her motherly instincts, Alice misses the part-time job. What kind of future is there for Jessica?

And Randy? They both have the desire and talent to go on. Let's not forget about the attorney. There is no way he will keep pushing that lawn mower. I am sure when he finishes his mowing, he rubs his hands and then yells out, "I'll sue those ba------s."

More information is coming out about the unaffected areas in northern Maine and our West Coast. Perhaps they can help us.

The anxiety level will reach a boiling point with the Randal's and others. For now Ben is finding some kindling wood, and Randy is polishing his Buick. Alice is keeping the family together, and insecure Jessica is on a mission to save the drunk.

In our family and in our little community, we have chosen the life-affirming position of old-fashioned values. The wrath of an EMP attack pushed us to this way of life in order to survive. Hopefully, with help of more of the horses, we can pull over the larger hills like the lust for power and around the ruts of bigotry hatred and selfishness. We will see. It's not 1776, but it should be interesting.

Printed in the United States
By Bookmasters